Esoteric Journey

Ron Mueller

Esoteric Journey

Books and Stories by Ron Mueller

The Door Series
The Door
Aliens We
The Endless Hole
The Swarm
Esoteric Journey
Why?

The Taelo Series
Taelo: The Early Years
Taelo: The Golden Feather
Taelo: Journey of Discovery
Taelo: Dangerous Passage
Taelo: Condor Clan Slingers
Taelo: Circumvention
Taelo: The Journey of Sages
Taelo: Collection
Taelo: Future Leaders Journey

A Taelo Story:
White Swan and Quiet Pheasant
The Child's Name
Floating Cloud
Quiet Rabbit
Busy Bee
Little Otter & Talking Wren
Broken Spear
Burley Bear & Meadow Flower
A Taelo Story Collection

Science Fiction
The Savitar Series:
Journey's End
Savitar
Confluence
Savitar Collection

Bram Nielson Series
The Fold
The Message
Fold Wormhole
Negative Fold
Ripples in Time
Bram Nielson Collection

Single Science Fiction Books:
Current Past and Future
The Event
Viajante 7

Ron Mueller

Fiction Series

The Alex Evercrest Series
The River Front
The Girl on The Grill
Missing
Maggot
Racist
Votive Candles
Windy City
Country Road
Pool of Blood
Sins of the Daughter
Alex Evercrest Heroin Collection
Body Parts
The Skull Collector
The Vanishing
The Shadow Fighter
Moonshine
Grief's Trajectory
The Magic Touch
Northern Lights
Alex Evercrest Collection Two
New Direction
A Family Affair

A Brian Oneil Novell
Hawaiian Phoenix
Moon Curser
Death Broker
Hawaiian Princesses

The Problem Solver Series
Solutions
Drug Lords
Border Crosser

Imagination by Courtney Huynh and Chloe Parker

Esoteric Journey
By: *Ron Mueller*

Around the World Publishing LLC
4914 Cooper Road Suite 144
Cincinnati, Ohio 45242-9998

This story is a work of fiction. Names, characters, places, and incidents either are products of the author's imagination or are used fictitiously. Any resemblance to actual events or locales or persons, living or dead, is entirely coincidental.

Esoteric Journey: © 2025

ISBN 13: 978-1-68223-935-3
ISBN 10: 1-68223-935-7

Distributed by Ingram
Cover Picture by: Koxae Sun @ShutterStock
Cover Design by: Ron Mueller

Ron Mueller

Esoteric Journey

Table of Content

Chapter 1: Panspermia   1

Chapter 2: The Outies   15

Chapter 3: Intergalactic Governance   27

Chapter 4: A Seed on Fertile Ground   39

Chapter 5: Return to the Quartet   47

Chapter 6: The Fourth Colony   55

Chapter 7: The Fifth Planet   69

Chapter 8: Technology Assimilation   85

Chapter 9: Focused Political Message   95

Chapter 10: The Source   107

Chapter 11: Tirayidi of Bintang   117

Chapter 12: Revolt   127

Chapter 13: Positive Change   137

Chapter 14: Meeting of the Minds   145

Chapter 15: Reawakening After Destruction   155

Chapter 16: Greening of Mirabiro   167

Chapter 17: Eighth Colony Challenge   175

Chapter 18: The Jomaoko   189

Chapter 19: Journey to the Peak   203

Chapter 20: More than a Gold Mine   217

Chapter 21: Completion and Next Steps   231

About the Author   241

Characters in the Story   242

Ron Mueller

1

Panspermia

I am Laki the historian that has researched the history of the United Intergalactic Worlds Organization. I begin my narrative on the many accomplishments of Five Star Admiral Joseph Pender Elsinger well into his spectacular career. He grew up on a Texan ranch, left to go to university and while there was given a death sentence when diagnosed with cancer. He was one of three persons to volunteer to be a guinea pig as a test for the viability of transmitting a human from one location to another through a device later given the moniker, the Door. He met and fell wildly in love with his wife to be, who was the first person to transit through the Door. She later became a Captain of one of the Cosmos Ships that was under his command. The story of his rise to his Five Star rank is a lengthy story in itself, my focus during this narrative is on his discovery of the eight other human colonies that were spread throughout the universe and his visit to my planet of origin.

The discovery of the first human colony was in response to that colonies broadcast for help. They faced extinction due to a dying star that they orbited. Their discovery surprised the Admiral and he made the decision to provide help.

1 Panspermia

He and his team sought and discovered another world for them and arranged for Earth to provide the support for them to transition to their new planet. It was not until the discovery of a second population of humans that the seeding of humans across the universe by superior beings came to he and his team.

Then he became focused on proving or disproving the theory that he and his team had zeroed in on.

He was a visionary that led his teams in a journey across the universe in his focused desire to prove a theory he had personally come to believe in whole heartedly. The numerous accounts written that highlight each step of his personal growth and the journeys of he and his team across the universe is a story worth understanding. So let me begin with the time when the concept about the spread of humanity throughout the universe first came to life and then to action taken by he and his team.

****

Bilian Phene a DNA analysist, assigned to lead the DNA comparison of the beings on Niam to those on Earth shared that the two populations were the exact duplicates.

Joe added that he felt that way as well. He then speculated that there might be other planets that had been seeded by some advanced civilization and the team needed to find a way to validated that idea.

Darian spoke up and said that he had a theory that the ancient Egyptians had left a message to that effect when they had built the Great Pyramid of Giza.

The meeting room went silent and Samantha asked why he had zeroed in on the Pyramid.

Esoteric Journey

He shared that recent analysis of the Great Pyramid had discovered it had eight points. He went on and added that the great pyramids construction demonstrated the knowledge of the circumference of the Earth, the distance between the Earth and the Sun, the distance between the Earth and the Moon and provided the means to measure the great precession cycle of twenty seven thousand, seven hundred, seventy two years. He shook his head and said that he doubted that all of that knowledge had been accumulated by people wandering the desert randomly building pyramids.

He went on to say that he was convinced that the humans that built the Great Pyramid of Giza were the descendants of the people that had been seeded to broaden the human population. And those doing the seeding were humans planting Human colonies.

Samantha chuckled and commented that she had wondered what the Endeavor's scientific officer had been doing.

Darian smiled and said that he had always been fascinated by the pyramids. He added that he was betting on eight base points and the one at the top being the race that had seeded that other planets.

Joe nodded and said that they should take Darian seriously and determine where to look for the next seeded planet.

Darian said that he figured that if they went out at the angle an eight sided base made and the same distance as Earth was from Niam they should find the next Earth like people.

H^3 shook his head and said that he could figure out the coordinates to use to locate the next point but the question was at what angle should that point be.

1 Panspermia

Lydia asked if the two suns position to the plane of the orbits of the two planets, Earth and Niam, might provide a clue to where they should look next.

The original forefathers might have planted them in a manner that provided an easy manner to find them. They may not have meant for the pyramid to be built but the people that were left on the planet had perhaps been provided the clues that would lead the Cosmos team to all the seeded planets and the seeding beings.

Tom nodded and said that it would take he, Linda and H^3 a few days before they determined the coordinates for their next Hole.

Bilian had listened to the dialogue and said that she was being blown away on how the Cosmos team functioned. She added that she hoped that her skill in DNA analysis would qualify her to join the next journey through the Hole.

Lacey smiled and said that if Bilian survived a cattle round up on Joe's ranch she could have a berth on her ship.

Joe laughed and said that Lacey was just trying to message him how cruel he treated all his personnel. He then ended the meeting and asked Tom to reconvene it when he, Linda and H^3 figured out where they were going.

Jackie had interviewed Lacey at Joe's request and realized that she was speaking with one of the most self-confident persons she had ever interviewed. She had reassured Joe that he should have no worries about the ex-President agreeing to a position as Captain of the newly built Cosmos Ambassador.

Esoteric Journey

She was surprised when Lacey called her and asked her to interview Bilian Phene to see if she would qualify to be on her ship. She took the opportunity to ask if she, herself, might be considered to join the crew. She had been part of the Door team from the very beginning and had been a part of the Hole team but always in an after the fact position. She really wanted to be at the point of action.

She got a provisional acceptance but was informed that she would need to pass the training all individuals underwent before they could be considered to be on board any of the Cosmos ships.

Tom, Linda and H^3 were pouring over the technical drawing of the Great Pyramid. The fact that it was a concave octagonal pyramid complicated their ability to locate the coordinates for the next Hole. They wondered if Niam was a corner point or if it was one of the concave points. If it was a concave point they would need to angle back out to a corner point. If it was a corner point they would need to angle inward to find the next planet.

Tom laughed as he took out a quarter and said that he was going to flip it. Heads Niam was a corner point, tails it was a concave point.

The quarter came up tails and Tom said that they were ready to reconvene the meeting and let Joe know the coordinates of the next hole.

In the meeting, when Joe found out how the coordinates had been determined he and the entire team laughed. He added that he had a new appreciation for the workings of the three most powerful minds in the world. That got a, "Voya…Voya…Voya" response from the team.

He reminded them that the next events were the commissioning of the USS Cosmos Ambassador and the practice of the four ships together before they made the next transit.

Darian said he had an on how to determine whether Niam was a concave or a corner point. He suggested that they check to see if there were stars located in across different galaxies that would fit the eight sides base of the Great Pyramid.

It was only a few days later that Tom offered to buy him a cold one because now he was sure that Niam was a concave point and he and H^3 were working on the coordinates of the next Hole but even better if they found the next planet they had the coordinates of all the stars where they would find the other five planets and that would as well give them the location of the ninth planet.

Joe said that it was great news and that in the next month or so they all would be the holding the qualification practice for the Cosmos Quartet.

The practice went well and Joe then gave the entire Quartet crew five days of leave before the Quartet transited through the next Hole.

He and Lydia headed directly to the ranch.

At dinner that evening Joe chewed slowly on a slice of tender salty, rare, steak with blue cheese melting across its surface as he sat and contemplated the diverse thinking that was flowing slowly through his mind.

Esoteric Journey

He did not have anything against conventional religions but he could not accept the biblical genealogies that the creation of the human was only six thousand years ago since that made Adam and Eve six thousand years young. Nor did he believe that the two of them were fifteen feet tall as was written in some ancient texts. That really messed with his mind.

His mother had taken him to the small Lutheran church in Canadian, Texas when he was young and he had been grounded in the New Testament with the belief that the Old Testament was the historic foundation but that his beliefs and practices should all come from the New Testament. His mind had balanced the situation out in a simple manner, Old Testament – Foundational History, New Testament – the way to live. The problem for him was that the timing of the old testament was mucked up.

His father and Uncle Ted were not avid church goers so Joe let most of the teaching in his younger years linger. Now he was being challenged by the discovery of people that were duplicates of Earthlings and a new and radical concept had taken hold. He was thinking well beyond the most accepted theory of biochemical evolution and focusing in on Panspermia. This was a mind expanding thought and tested all his beliefs.

He took a sip of his lemonade and thought about the fact that humans may have originated elsewhere in the universe and might have been transported to Earth.

1 Panspermia

He understood Panspermia to be the concept that life originated elsewhere in the universe and reached Earth through space travel. In the case he was contemplating people were placed on Earth by advanced extraterrestrial beings that had made that journey many eons before. This made him a Pre-Adamist in his thinking and put him well outside of most conventional thought.

He understood Panspermia (from Ancient Greek πᾶν (pan) 'all' and σπέρμα (sperma) 'seed') was the hypothesis that life exists throughout the Universe and could be distributed by space dust, meteoroids, asteroids, comets, and planetoids, as well as by spacecraft carrying unintended contamination by microorganisms, known as directed panspermia. He was also at the edge of Panspermiatic thinking in that he was thinking about the directed panspermia that had placed life on multiple planets not by accident but by beings with the specific intent of expanding their species. He was accepting the thinking of Leslie Ogel and Nobel prize winner Francis Cick who published the idea of "directed panspermia", meaning an advanced being sent life to Earth to fulfill a purpose. He was one step beyond that when he envisioned a specific space vessel delivering the beings to Earth and he was envisioning thousands of humans being delivered.

As he thought about how far out his thinking was and that it was based on the Pyramid of Gaza that had eight base points with a ninth point being the top of the pyramid, he realized that he was stretching the Rare Earth hypothesis that argues that planets with life, like Earth, were exceptionally rare.

He was virtually refuting very famous people who argued that Earth was a rocky planet in a typical planetary system, located in a non-exceptional region of a common spiral galaxy. He was instead taking the position that Earth was special in its location and that similar planets existed in other specific special locations in the universe that he needed to discover.

Joe continued his ruminating as he thought about the other theories of the origin of life. He had looked into the theory that life began in ice, another that life began in clay, there was the RNA theory of life's origin and there was the theory that life had begun in the deep sea vents.

He was also aware that for at least a hundred years, physicists, cosmologists, and philosophers have pondered the possibility that Earth and the people on it are far from unique. It seemed that scientists today believed it was very likely there were infinite versions of Earth like planets and beings like earthlings out there somewhere.

Joe looked around the table, realized that no one was talking and everyone was looking at him. He wondered what he had done to attract attention.

Lydia smiled and said that she had never seen him attack a steak with such vengeance and animosity and asked him what was running through his mind.

Uncle Ted asked if his steak deserved such rough treatment.

1 Panspermia

Joe laughed and said that he was being possessed by the cosmic powers mentioned in Ephesians 6:12, "cosmic powers over this present darkness...spiritual forces found in heavenly places." He added that more specifically he was thinking about other Earth like planets out in the universe and the concept of Panspermia.

Uncle Ted chuckled and asked if Panspermia was a brand of kitchen pots and pans that he had not heard of and if so he was willing to buy a set if they allowed him to prepare steaks that Joe did not try to brutalize.

Once again Joe laughed and said that he loved the steak and he was not talking about pots and pans but about the universe and the beings that had seeded the Earth.

His father spoke up and added that he had never been a devout religionist but it sounded as if he was on the edge of the accepted theories of life on Earth. He went on to say that it sound like he might need to put up high razor topped fences to keep all the devout Baptists, Catholics, and most other religions from storming the ranch.

Lydia nodded and said that once they finished dessert she and Joe should do some heavy duty riding so his brain could get back into the rhythm of the saddle and his feet would once again be in the stirrups of a horse pounding the ground versus, riding a ghost horse somewhere up in the clouds.

Joe smiled and said that living on the ranch was the reason he had not so far been disqualified from his position but unless his theories hit home he would soon be questioned about where he was taking the Cosmos Quartet.

A few days later, back on the Cosmos Voyager, Joe called a meeting of his inner group to discuss his thinking. He asked if Tom, Linda, H[3] and Darian had decided if the planet they had found was an innie or an outie.

Darian spoke up and said that he wanted to explain because if H[3] were to explain none of them would understand. He added that simply put the planet they had found was an innie and the next targeted star should be the location of an outie planet.

Joe let them know that their idea of finding eight base planets and a ninth as the origin of the other eight put all of them on the very fringe of any concepts of how life emerged on Earth. They were so far on the fringe that he added they were way outside all the ball parks of any sport. He added that Jackie might finally declare that he had gone over the edge and order a straitjacket for him.

Lacey chuckled and said that if she had followed conventional thinking she would still be stuck on the ground. She would rather follow his unconventional thinking and go where no one else had gone before. She chuckled when that got a groan from everyone in the meeting. After a pause she continued and added that everywhere that Joe had led them, they had found beings of many different kinds. It would not surprise her that at some point in time a superior race decided to plant their species in multiple locations as a way to ensure its continuation. She was ready to take Joe's orders and go on an adventure that stretched her and all their imaginations.

1 Panspermia

Samantha said that this journey would be different in from the others they had so far gone on because they were now four cosmos space vessels that were flying together and they had decided that all four ship commanders would rotate and be the primary Captain on a regular basis. Only when they were initially going through the Hole would one of the captains directly command all four ships. This concept was also being extended to each of the operating systems to allow a more flexible amount of time for everyone during the journey.

Joe commented that he liked the idea and suggested that on the time off, everyone be given the opportunity to do one thing they wanted to do but they must also put in extra time doing some sort of physical routine. He added that he would participate in the rotation and at that time one of the Captains would take his seat.

He then asked if Tom had the coordinates of the next Hole.

Tom let him know that they were programmed in.

Joe asked if Lakland control was ready for the departure of the Cosmos Quartet.

Jorge chuckled and said they were ready and ready to listen to the music of the Quartet.

Lacey laughed said that the music would not be played by a quartet it was going to be the Marcha Radetzky by Johann Strauss and everyone should clap along. It had been selected to thank everyone for having made this next phase of their journey out to the beyond possible.

Esoteric Journey

As the music hit each of the final passages, the Hole cannon fired, next the cleaning lasers went through, the protection lasers followed and then the Cosmos Quartet disappeared and the clapping stopped.

There was a cheer from ground control and Jorge knew that Joe was off to a very different journey. He wondered if it would work out as expected. He also knew that so far every journey had entailed adversaries that either panicked and attacked or attacked on purpose. In either case Joe had managed to have his team come out on top. Jorge was sure that Joe had practiced the Quartet long and hard enough that they would not easily be defeated.

Once through the hole Joe had Tom looking for the star that would most likely have the desired planet circling it. He knew that now the innie or outie question would be answered. He waited patiently before giving any additional orders other than to hold defensive positions and stay on alert.

Tom, H^3 and Linda were frantically looking for the star and planets circling it that would answer the question. There were three stars that were in position that would make the answer an outie as they hope it would be. Each star had multiple planets and several around each star were in the goldilocks zone. They split up the evaluation and each of them took on one star and rapidly evaluated the planets for advanced civilizations.

H^3 was the one that suddenly let out a "Voya…Voya…Voya" as he pumped his hand up and down. It's an outie he shouted as he stood up and pointed to the sixth planet circling a yellow star.

1 Panspermia

Yara came over to him and gave him a hug and suggested he sit back down and set up the coordinates that would get them near the planet to see if the people there were indeed human.

Tom kept quiet as the coordinates for the planet that H^3 had identified were determined. Just before the Cosmos Quartet was to make the transit. He quietly suggested that he had a competitor planet that could also be their quest. He suggested that they spend more time to penetrate each of the planets to determine which one they wanted to go to first.

There was a quiet moment before Joe took the opportunity to speak up. He said that as the umpire, referee, and ring master of the team he was calling a time out. They would take the time to do a closer analysis of the two planets and might visit both to see if they had found two different intelligent species in two nearby stars.

He said that everyone should take a break, visit the mess hall, enjoy the dinner that was being offered and then follow the standard rotation schedule.

He called a meeting of his inner team. This time Jackie, now their resident psychologist and Billian their DNA specialist were include. He let them know that they would visit the planet that won out by being the most likely to have their human counterparts. He was at the edge of anxiety and was hoping that they indeed were on the right trail. If they found their counterparts, then they would have to revise how they perceived the history of Earth.

Billian commented that she was personally about to find out how sane she thought she was.

2

<u>**The Outies**</u>

The discovery of the second planet populated by humans was a critical and catalytic step in the creation of the United Intergalactic Human Worlds Organization. Laki realized that the Admiral had leveraged the team's understanding of Earth's history and his dynamic way to energize his team to the successfully predict the location of the third human world. It was a fluke that when he led the vessel that combine four of the Cosmos ships into one sphere called the Cosmos Quartet there were two potential planetary candidates that might have humans on them. These two planets each circled a different star. The closest star was the one with the human population. The second star also had intelligent life and is an important part of the Admiral's story that entails a battle that tested the capabilities of the Cosmos Quartet team and created a slight delay in the discovery of the remaining human seed colonies.

Up to this point the Admiral had rescued one human population and had discovered a second human population. In both situations the two discoveries gave a new perspective into the societal conditions on each of the three planets and surfaced the question as to why Earth was an outlier in the aggressiveness of its societies.

2 The Outies

The two discovered human worlds had societies that did not have the societal differences that caused the wars that was woven into Earth's historic fabric. The Admiral concluded that Earth was at one end while the two discovered worlds were at the other end of human social interactions. He also concluded that on Earth he belonged to the part of society that was on the "live and let live" side of the emotional spectrum. But I digress, let me bring the focus back to the discovery of the third human settled world.

****

The Sphere was sitting stationary as if making observations. Zacker was looking at the screen in the team room as he and his team analyzed its actions. Its appearance had surprised he and his team in that it did not come across the void but just suddenly appeared. He had played back the recorded visuals multiple times. One moment the area was empty then a series of rockets appeared and fired lasers inwardly and then an equal number of rockets appeared and positioned themselves in the same spherical configuration but took no action. Then an oblong object that seemed to have no purpose positioned itself to the edge of the sphere of lasers. A few seconds later the small sphere appeared at the center of all the lasers. He had watched the video multiple times before taking any action. He was not clear what he would recommend to the Gaja Leadership Council.

He communicated the appearance of the sphere to the leadership council who activated all the defense forces. They instructed him to monitor the alien vessel and to let them know if it made any hostile moves.

He was aware that the rather new space exploration unit was on the verge of launching the first satellite and he was also aware that the defense force did not have weapons that went as far out as the alien sphere was located. He felt constrained and hoped that the aliens were inclined to be friendly and only to be explorers seeking to establish contact.

He had his team using the most powerful ground based five-hundred-meter aperture spherical reflector dish to zoom in on the alien sphere and was able to see that it seemed to be made up of four separate units that were operating as one. Each unit was rotating and his team was able to theorize that the rotation created almost the same gravitational force that was experienced on Gaja. It surprised him that the aliens would be generating a force that was so close to what Gaja had as gravity. He wondered where they had come from and what their physical features might be.

Zacker noted the fact that the entire sphere had stopped rotating and only one of the rotating wheel sections was pointed at the planet. With a higher magnification of the sphere, he was able to see that there seemed to be several physical instruments that to him looked like telescopes. This made him wonder if the sphere was looking back at him and Gaja to study it as he was studying them.

And he would be surprised to learn later that indeed he was being watched by Tom, H^3, Linda and the rest of the personnel on the Cosmos Quartet. They were carefully scanning each of the seven planets that circled the star that they were referring to as the Outie Star system.

The planet closest to the star was similar to Venus and was not in the goldilocks zone. The second planet was in the very middle of the zone and the third planet was out at the edge of the goldilocks zone but looked like a frozen ocean world. Tom utilized all four of the Quartet's telescopes to create a more powerful one. This let him zoom in on outie planet two. He was surprised to see what reminded him of the Arecibo Observatory in Puerto Rico. He announced that he was sure that there were intelligent beings on the outie planet number two and they might be sophisticated enough to be studying the Cosmos Quartet.

H^3 commented that he had been able to make out what he took as planes flying and cities that seemed to be as large as Atlanta or New York. So, the beings were definitely technologically advanced.

Joe thanked Tom and H^3 and asked that Kashanti beam down his picture with his empty hand raised as a sign of friendship.

Zacker almost fell out of his seat when the picture of the alien came on the screen. He could have been looking at his brother in law. He looked like anyone on Gaja.

He dropped everything and contacted the Gaja leadership council head and showed him the picture. He added that he interpreted the picture with the raised empty hand to indicate a desire to be friendly. He verified that he should reply with a similar picture in response.

Joe and everyone on the Quartet let out a call of "Voya... Voya...Voya" when the picture was flashed up on the screen. They all knew that they had found the planet that verified the theory that humans were indeed seeded around the universe.

The cheering was followed by a continuous discussion of what this meant and the impact of the history of Earth.

Joe laughed and said that they needed to table that discussion and focus on setting up communication with the people on the planet.

He asked Kashanti to send a series of pictures that showed and had labels for a male, female, children, eye colors and start the process of establishing communication with the beings on the planet. He also wanted to know what the beings called their star and their planet. Kashanti let him know that his team would spend every moment to get the communication at as high a level as possible.

Joe then called a meeting of his leadership team. He suggested that they retrieve the Door module and proceed slowly toward the planet.

Lydia asked if anyone had any issues with what Joe was suggesting.

Samantha suggested that they repeatedly send out the visual of Joe holding up his hand as they slowly approached the planet.

Joe agreed that they do exactly that. He then gave the order for the Cosmos Quartet to move slowly toward planet two.

Kashanti announced that as close as he could translate the pictures and the language the planet was called Gaja and the star was Bintang.

Yara smiled and said that now she could quit laughing at calling the planet an outie.

On Gaja, Zacker watched as the sphere retrieved the object that he had been calling a cube. He noted that all the lasers were retrieved as well. Those actions actually calmed him since it seemed that the function of the lasers had been defensive.

He was somewhat alarmed as he watched the sphere begin a slow movement towards Gaja. At the same time his communication specialist informed him that the sphere was repeatedly sending the picture of the individual with a raised hand. Since there was not much that he could do about the situation he gave instructions that they should reply with his picture and his hand raised.

He did notify the leadership council leader about the situation. He was asked to find out whether the beings in the approaching space sphere were the ones that had long ago seeded Gaja. This was a piece of history that now made Zacker wonder if indeed the aliens were actually the people of the legend that described how Gajans had come to be on the planet. They truly might be the answer to a long held belief of everyone on Gaja.

Joe and the rest of the leadership team were not surprised when they received a series of pictures that had the planet Gaja showing people being lowered from the sky to its surface from the Cosmos Quartet. He suggested that they reply with a picture that crossed out the people going down and instead had a picture of the Earth with him on the surface and picture of the Gajan standing on the surface of their planet.

Kashanti suggested that they follow up with a picture of the Bintang solar system and the Earth's solar system diagrams showing where they came from. He added that he and his team were already making great strides in defining the alphabet and the numbering system that was used on Gaja. He said that his team had sent the English alphabet down to the planet with pictures and were making amazingly rapid progress in getting the Gaja equivalent.

He shared the fact that what they were zeroing in on was very similar to the Phoenician alphabetic script with distinct letters for vowels as well as consonants. He said that it was so close to the Latin alphabet that in a few days they would be able to have a translation module that would allow full conversations to take place.

On Baja, Zacker was very pleased with the progress that his team was making with the beings that he now understood to be the equals of every one on Gaja and not the beings that Gajans historically considered the beings that had seeded the planet.

However, it was clear to him that though the person being shown was shown as a brother, the person up in the sphere was sitting in space, had mysteriously appeared, was able to move about at will and now sat in a stationary position above Gaja. This was a display of such superior technology that he wondered how it was all possible.

He eagerly waited until he would be able to ask questions that might provide some understanding that for him was for the moment lacking. For him it had an impact that was hard to immediately process. He had spent his life working to get out in space. He and all the members of his immediate family were all space enthusiasts.

He wondered if now there might be a leap frog in the ability for Gajan's to get out into space. Perhaps he would live to see many of his dreams come to life.

On the Quartet, Tom was analyzing the cities that appeared on Gaja. He commented that based on what he was seeing, the planet had been developed in a much greener way than what had occurred on Earth. He added that it appeared that a few Gajans got around by using flying vehicles just like the sci-fi movies on Earth but given the size of the cities he speculated that much of the in city transit was underground. He then went on with his speculation that the transportation to other cities was also underground because there did not seem to be any air transportation between them. If that was the case then there must be massive tunnels beneath the oceans that like the Earth was eighty percent of the planet's surface.

Joe facilitated a meeting to discuss how they should handle Gaja and when they would continue to the fourth planet of the eight they were seeking.

Lydia suggested that they establish contact, enter into a discussion with the beings on the planet, get approval to put a Door module into orbit around the planet and get the Intergalactic Diplomacy Corps to continue to develop the ongoing relationship with the planet.

Linda agreed that was a good approach and wondered if they would be able to accomplish that in a thirty day period at each planet. If the greeting at each planet was friendly as it was at the moment they could also operate at a lower staffing level and allow part of the crew time off. During the time off she suggested that the personnel rotate back to Earth.

Lacey agreed that bringing in the Diplomatic Corps as soon as possible was the way to go. She could get that organized and set up with the folks that were currently running the organization. She added that now that they were on the trail around the base, the Diplomatic Corps could be hiring and getting their staff increased to match the number of worlds they would be working with. She added that initially the people interfacing with each planet would be small but by the time they were done that organization would grow significantly.

Joe had listened to his team and was in agreement with most of what they were suggesting. He knew that he would need to return to Earth to work through the details on a firsthand basis. He was now sure that they would find the other planets that housed humans and most likely find additional other types of intelligent beings. He was also aware that the first connection had been made because the beings on the first planet, the Nivians were in desperate need and accepted the fact that Earth could provide the needed support to save all the people on a planet threatened by a dying sun.

Gaja was a world that had some technology that would be very useful on Earth. They also seemed to lack war armament or missiles. This seemed to indicate a history that would be very different from the turbulent one that Earth had. He accepted this as a hopeful sign for the subsequent worlds that the Cosmos Quartet would find. That hope was not going to reduce his preparedness for interacting with a world more like Earth that might have a very negative reaction to the arrival of the Cosmos Quartet.

He figured he had found two of the easier planets to work with. He was sure that he would find that the spectrum of what the Quartet would face would span across a relationship spectrum from the easy, the moderate to the hard to get along with. He needed to communicate this to the President and to get an agreement on how to handle each situation.

He was sure that it was time to establish the Organization of Intergalactic Governance that was an independent body separated from Earth's control that eventually would have representatives from every world that had so far been discovered. He envisioned it to be organized along the lines of The United Nations but having a military arm that would be filled primarily by the Cosmos Fleet. He currently felt that there should be three permanent members on the Intergalactic Governance Organization that had a veto on what the organization was undertaking and doing across the galaxies. Earth would have one of those positions and eventually the other two positions would be defined based on the strength of the organization and the need to create balance.

He envisioned leading his team in defining, designing, and staffing the framework of such an organization. It needed to rapidly get its feet on the ground so it would be ready when they approached planet number nine at the apex of the eight sided pyramid.

He needed to act and he let everyone know that he was going to act to establish the Organization of Intergalactic Worlds and they should stay in place and continue to establish solid communication with the Gajans.

2 The Outies

3

Intergalactic Governance

I learned that the concept of the United Intergalactic Worlds Organization came to the Admiral as he contemplated going on to find the fourth planet with humans. He returned to Earth to plant the seed that would result in the organization to take root. He returned to the base of his support and to his roots on the ranch on which he had grown up. He returned to enroll the President of the United States.

His two longtime supporters Rear Admiral Jorge Martinez and Rear Admiral Jerald Delaney provided a supportive sounding board that gave him the confidence to engage the President.

His brief stay at the ranch provided the grounding that he always sought. The advice that he got from the person every one called Uncle Ted and from his father Trey went a long way in providing the feeling that he was on the right track. His ride across the vast terrain of the ranch on his horse Yin that was a part of his love affair with his wife Lydia, whose horse was named Yang gave him the surge of confidence that he needed to keep going on the quest to get an organization that would unite humans across the universe.

He knew he was at the boundary of what was going to be accepted on Earth. He did not want to have it miss the opportunity to propel the beauty and the good that Earth had to share with the other worlds. He wanted to ensure the human population that had been seeded came together in a common, warm embracing intergalactic society. He envisioned that eventually people of each world would visit each other's home planets when they vacationed. Again, my enthusiasm makes me diverge because I know that his vision has been achieved. I have personally vacationed on three of the planets and plan to continue until I have worked my way around the base. I live on the ninth planet that the Admiral visited. That visit was a shock to my world and is a story of its own. Let me constrain my enthusiasm and again focus on the Admiral and his team.

****

Joe's return via the Door surprised Jorge and Jerry. They were both notified as soon as Joe stepped out of the Door module. They rode over together to the Door Building and greeted Joe as he exited. They could tell by the fact that he was in full dress uniform that he had come back via the Door for a specific reason otherwise he would have donned his ranch outfit. After a formal salute, Jorge listened as Joe said that he wanted to share what his current journey was discovering and what he wanted to do that would have a significant impact on the way the Intergalactic Space Force would operate and who it would report to.

This certainly was not on the minds of either of them.

Jorge nodded and said that it was currently after five. He suggested that the three of them gather at his residence, enjoy dinner, and then spend the evening doing what Joe wanted.

Joe chuckled and said that he had left the Voyager after breakfast and a meeting with the four Cosmos Captains. He would add tracking time across the universe as a task that he would ask Tom to solve.. He said that dinner at Jorge's place sounded great. He would go to his residence, change into his civilian clothes, and walk over for dinner. He saluted Jorge and Jerry, was getting ready to go to his place and realized that he did not have a vehicle to take him.

Jorge smiled and said that it was more than time that Joe needed to get his bearings on. He said that he should sit in the front passenger seat and the two of them would drop him off at his place so he would not have to lose any more time.

Joe nodded and said that it was hard to make the adjustment from being on the Voyager and being back on the base.

Once at his residence he took a quick shower, put on his jeans, and a sports shirt pulled on his boots and walked out of the house. He was surprised to be greeted by three armed Space Force Marine guards. They all saluted him and then dropped the salute when he said, "at ease." He smiled and asked who had notified them that he was in his residence.

The Sergeant Major replied that Rear Admiral Delaney had instructed them to walk with him to Rear Admiral Martinez's home and then stand by to be available when it was time to escort the Admiral back.

Joe nodded and said that the three of them should follow the Rear Admiral's orders but they should do it in a casual manner. He did not need them to march him to the Martinez's residence but would welcome a casual walk while they each told him about themselves and their experience in the Space Corps.

Once they got to the Jorge's house, Joe suggested that they sit down in the foyer and he would arrange for them to enjoy a great meal while they waited for him to return to his residence.

Joe proceeded to the kitchen where he found Jorge and Jerry sitting, sipping on an iced tea as they watched Jimena put the finishing touches on three racks of St. Louis Cut Ribs that had been sent by Uncle Ted to her.

Joe knew that the ribs were the meatiest and most flavorful part of the rib rack. Uncle Ted always had the tips removed so they formed a perfect rectangular rack. He also spiced them before sending them to Jimena. She looked at him and asked how many ribs he wanted. He smiled and said that he wanted nine ribs.

Jimena laughed and said that if he ate nine ribs he would need to be taken home via the hospital.

Joe nodded and said that he had three Space Force Marine guards who one of his two rear admirals had assigned to guard him sitting in the foyer who he had promised dinner.

Jimena said that if they were going eat her ribs they needed to be brought into the kitchen, sit down at the table with the rest of them because she was not going to have anyone sitting in the foyer eating.

Jerry put up his hand and said that he would bring them in.

Jorge smiled and said that he would set the table.

After getting a hug from Jimena, Joe helped set the table.

Jerry returned with the three guards who had left all their gear except for their weapons in the foyer. Jerry pointed to the entry area as the place for them to place their weapons.

Jorge sat them down on one end of the table and offered them iced tea to drink.

Jimena brought them each a bowl of salad and said they should relax and enjoy themselves because they were about to enjoy one of the best meals that she knew how to prepare.

Joe sat down across from the three and introduced each of them and gave a brief back ground depiction of each of them. He smiled when Jimena asked if he knew the three. He nodded and said that each of them had become his friend as they walked over from his residence and each of them had accepted an invitation out to the ranch.

After dinner, Jorge suggested that they go to the family room to have the discussion about why Joe had returned.

Jimena let the three guards know that part of the duty of guarding the Admiral was to help in cleaning the table, rinsing, and putting the dishes in the dishwasher and in general getting everything in the kitchen ready for the next day. After that they should sit and enjoy some cookies and milk.

Joe was walking out of the kitchen but stopped, smiled, and commented that he had forgotten to let them know about the price of the dinner and then followed Jorge to the family room.

Jerry chuckled, commented that he was curious what he would hear about the dinner via the grape vine.

Jorge replied that what he was going to get was a lot of volunteers wanting the duty of guarding the Admiral. He then said that he really wanted to hear why Joe had thought it important enough to come back to Earth while the Cosmos Quartet remained somewhere in the Universe.

Joe began by reminding Jorge that before leaving they had discussed the fringe theory that humans had been seeded on Earth by some beings that had the capability to do so. He pointed out that the Great Pyramid at Giza was a record left by the early humans that described the number and position of similar seeded planets. He went on to point out that there were three Cosmos ships focused on relocating eight billion Nivians to their new planet who had an ancient legend about being placed on their current planet by superior beings.

He paused for a moment and reminded them that his Quartet team had put it all together and predicted where the next seeded planet would be. He had used that prediction to set the coordinates for the Hole that the Quartet had gone through as they departed.

Jorge put up his hand and quietly said that a third planet of human like beings had been found.

Joe nodded.

Jerry shook his head and said that he was glad that he was not a devout believer in how religion had interpreted the history of Earth.

After a brief pause, Joe said that having three planets of humans was enough to convince him of the seeding theory and that he would take the Quartet on to find all of the seeded planets and then he would locate the ninth seeding planet and go there.

Jorge nodded and commented that he did not think that coming back to Earth to share that information was the reason that Joe had for coming back.

Jimena walked in with a tray that had three cups, a pot of tea and an assortment of fruit and put it down on the coffee table. She looked around and when she got a nod from each of the three she poured a cup of tea as she declared that it was a lemon mint tea that had no caffein. She smiled and added that she had chosen fruit over cookies because she knew Joe was watching his figure. Then as she was leaving she said goodnight and that she was going to go to bed and do a little reading before going to sleep. She added that she had left the three guards in the kitchen with a plate of cookies as well as a bowl of fruit.

Joe picked up his cup of tea, picked up a large strawberry took a bite and after swallowing, he replied to Jorge that he had come back to get the ball rolling on establishing the United Intergalactic Worlds Organization. He said that he wanted this organization to be organized similarly to the UN but to also have a defense force made up of the seven Cosmos Ships.

He wanted to get the President to set up the organization and get it started so that as he discovered all the planets that had humans on them, it would bring that planet in and establish the relationships necessary to have the organization functioning.

Jerry shook his head and said that it was lucky that he was not Catholic, like Jorge, because not only did everything that Joe and his team had discovered put all previous thinking on its head but it challenged most religious beliefs.

Jorge nodded; said they should focus on the reason Joe had returned. He said that establishing an organization to bring the nine planets into one mutually beneficial organization made lots of sense. He added that it would be an honor to be part of the team that led the establishment of such an entity. He smiled and said that he would deal with his own enlightenment about the implications associated with Joe's findings as he went along. He like every thinking person would need to make the adjustment to how they interpreted Earth's human history.

Joe shook his head and said that he and Lydia had been discussing exactly that. Intellectually he had no problem with the Cosmos journey he was on but personally it affected every religious belief that he had ever held. He smiled and asked, "Where is my mother that I always looked up into the sky to address?"

Jorge returned his smile and replied that she was exactly where she had always been and he was flying out there with her in his heart.

Joe looked at the grandfather clock whose bright brass pendulum was clicking back and forth and realized that it was close to midnight. He smiled and said that it was time for him to head to the ranch so he could enjoy Uncle Ted's special cubed ham pancakes with butter and slathered in Maple syrup that Samantha had personally made.

He sent a text to Uncle Ted and his father letting them know that he was flying to the ranch. He then went to the kitchen and let the three guards know that he was ready to head to the ranch.

Jerry had come with Joe and let the three know that they had the next few days off and could go with the Admiral to the ranch where they would do whatever the Admiral wanted.

Joe walked out and was surprised as he watched a van approach and stop in front of Jorge's residence.

Jorge said to give the President his best and if he agreed to Joe's idea, Joe should volunteer he and Jerry to lead the organization effort.

Joe smiled and said he would do exactly that so he and Jerry had better be ready for their next big headache that he would make sure would land in their lap.

Jorge and Jerry stood by the front door and watched Joe and the three Space Corps Marines get into the van. Jorge commented that Joe seemed to be a change catalyst.

Jerry commented that he agreed and added that the change always was very different than one would expect and they should prepare themselves for whatever might come their way.

3 Intergalactic Governance

Joe's dad looked at the text that he had received. He smiled, then sent a smiley face in reply. He then sent a text to Ted letting him know that Joe would be at breakfast. He was already in bed and did and planned to stay there until it was time for breakfast.

When the hilo landed it was just after one in the morning. Joe thanked the two pilots and invited them to breakfast later that morning when they brought the three marines that he had invited to spend a few days on the ranch. He went into the house, to his bedroom and fell across his bed. He lay there for a moment and then took off his clothes and climbed under the sheets. He fell asleep thinking of pancakes, melting butter and maple syrup.

The next morning the sun woke him. He got up, took a nice hot shower, brushed his teeth and after shaving went downstairs. When he walked into the kitchen Uncle Ted greeted him and his father offered him a cup of coffee. He had just finished his first cup of coffee when the sound of the hilo caught their attention. Joe said that he had invited three Intergalactic Marines and the two hilo pilots to breakfast. The Marines would stay for while he was there but the pilots would leave after breakfast.

Uncle Ted laughed and said that it was lucky for them that he had plenty of pancake mix and some great sausage for their breakfast.

Joe added that the three Marines had been invited to spend a couple of days and they should stay in the guest rooms in the ranch hand bunk area. He wanted them to get the feel of being cowhands so they should also be put to work.

His father asked why he had returned without Lydia.

Joe let him know that Lydia and the rest of the team were out at the third planet populated by humans.

The kitchen was quiet for a few seconds.

His father suggested that after breakfast the three of them go sit on the veranda and he could share what such a discovery meant.

3 Intergalactic Governance

4

A Seed on Fertile Ground

It is recorded that just before meeting with the US President the Admiral spent a few days on the ranch where he had grown up discussing his thoughts with his father and the person he and everyone called Uncle Ted. Their discussion seems to have been centered around the idea that there were a total of eight human seed colonies and the human seeder planet. I need to be transparent in my writing in that I am a citizen of that seeding planet. For years I have studied the records as I took a journey of my own digging into the Admirals accomplishments. He was a person with many facets but with one consistent and fundamental centering bedrock belief and that was that all beings should be respected and treated as equals. He as an individual was able to extend that belief to the tremendously diverse beings that he and his team had discovered. He extended this belief by forming an organization that from the beginning was charged with establishing social connections with each of the nine interstellar, human populations. I was even more impressed by the fact that he expanded that organizations charter to include beings of very different physical characteristics and social norms.

But once again I digress.

4 A Seed on Fertile Ground

My intent in this chapter is to highlight how he enrolled the US President in establishing the United Intergalactic Worlds Organization.

His first stop was to discuss the concept with his father and the person he considered his second father even though he called him Uncle Ted. They discussed the concept and together they had questioned their common belief that the Admiral's mother was in heaven. They concluded that she traveled with all of them in their hearts and it was Joe that ensured that she also resided in heaven.

I am personally moved that the three of them agreed that the Admiral's mother indeed was in the heavens and he was traveling with her in his heart. This seemed to bond me more to all three of them and especially to the Admiral.

The Admiral went on to meet with and solidly convince the President that such an organization should be established. The President had an upcoming election that he was sure to win and he promised the Admiral four more years of solid support and accepted the Admirals recommendation to have the two Intergalactic Rear Admirals Jorge Martinez and Gerald Delaney organize and staff the United Intergalactic Worlds Organization. I truly admire the Admirals visionary perspective and his ability to enroll leaders with such strong support and commitment to action.

****

The veranda was exactly the atmosphere that suited Joe. It was the location where he had heard many of Uncle Ted's or his father's stories. It provided him the backdrop that allowed him to unconsciously share his thoughts in a free and open manner.

He shared the fact that he had found the universe filled with many intelligent life forms. In fact, the number and variation of physical features had surprised him. He shared that growing up he had learned that intelligent life was very sparse throughout the universe. His explorations and the fact that those explorations crossed multi-billions of miles had proven the sparsity theory of intelligence was wrong. It seemed to him to be the common outcome of the billions of years the universe had been in existence.

He had come to appreciate the fact that the Hole technology allowed he and his team to instantaneously leap across those billions of miles and explore the universe in what could only be described as expeditions that allowed he and his team to experience the diversity that seemed to be the common model.

He then shared the details of his current journey of verifying a theory that he and his team shared. He explained that finding the first planet with beings that were duplicates of the people on Earth had triggered him to have his team investigate the possibility that the people on Earth and the second planet were indeed the same and that both had been placed on the planets as a means of spreading the human species across the universe.

He smiled and said that the shape of Pyramid of Giza had provided the road map he had his Cosmos ship following.

Uncle Ted interrupted to ask how a pyramid built by the pharaohs could possibly be linked to his current journey across the universe and was Joe trying to outdo his story telling.

Joe nodded, agreed that it seemed really impossible that the pyramid built more than four thousand six hundred years ago would be the road map for a journey across the universe but in fact it was. It turned out that H^3 had penetrated the design of the pyramid closely enough and identified that the pyramid was considered to have eight sides and had used that knowledge to predict where in the Universe the third planet that the Cosmos Quartet had just located and it was another planet with human like beings. Joe smiled and said that he would never try to outdo his Uncle in story telling but this time reality was indeed telling a story that rivaled him.

His father put up his hand, shook his head and said that what he was saying also challenged all the religious beliefs on Earth.

Joe nodded and said that indeed it did. He emphasized that all the writings were based on humans of their times recording the stories being passed down to them through multiple generations and finally at some point being written down.

He smiled and reminded his father of the game they had played on one scout camping trip where he had sent down the message that everyone could have an ice cream and by the time it went mouth to ear through the ten scouts the last scout reported what he had heard that he should stand up and scream, and he did.

His father laughed and said that he remembered that very well because that screamer was now sitting on his veranda and whispering a story in his ear that was very hard for him to accept.

Joe nodded and said that he had found it very hard to accept but the discovery of the third planet with humans on it had convinced him that in fact he would be going on and finding five more planets with humans on them. He went on and added that the fact that the oldest recorded languages only went back four thousand years and yet scholars had traced language back fifty thousand years. So, the records were sparse and patchy and what they thought of as fact might have followed the same path as the boy scout game.

He was counting on solidifying his current search for the nine human planets by following an ancient pyramid and the calculations to determine where to find them on his teams superb capability to find the stars and the planets where they should be found base on that ancient map.

Uncle Ted chuckled and said that from now on he and Trey would be the ones sitting on the Veranda listening to him tell the stories.

Joe shook his head and said that he was not the story teller and would never dream of competing with him but this time reality was giving all three of them a shock. He had returned to share what he had learned with them because he was looking for their guidance.

His father smiled and commented that he was not sure what sort of guidance he and Ted could give him.

Joe smiled and said that he had a meeting with the President to share a vision of how the worlds with intelligent beings should be brought together and managed.

4 A Seed on Fertile Ground

He wanted the opinions of the two most level thinking men he knew to give him their opinion on the idea of establishing the United Intergalactic Worlds Organization that would be charged with managing the relationships between the nine human planets and all other beings that he and his team discovered. He wanted that organization to establish and ensure a peaceful, fruitful interaction between all the planets. He wanted it to be similar to the UN but also have an enforcement arm made up of the Cosmos ships that would ensure a peaceful relationship.

Uncle Ted nodded and said that seemed like a good idea to get agreement to. That way there would be a way for all planets to establish relationships in an organized and peaceful manner.

His father put his hand on his and asked him where, if there was no heaven, they should think where his mother was.

Joe put his other hand on top of his father's and had to hold back a tear as he said that heaven was in their minds, love was in their hearts and that let him have his mother with him out in space in both heaven and his heart. She had been with him out there from the start and she flew with him to every new star and had been with him on every discovery. He added that for him nothing had changed with the discoveries that he had so far made.

His father put his other hand on top and said that made so much sense that it allowed him to accept the fact that most of his previous beliefs seemed to be taking spin as he processed what had been shared.

He then patted Joe's hand and said that setting up the organizations he had in mind made great sense and would most likely lead to a peaceful gathering of all nine human populations and any other intelligent species found. He liked the way that his son was extending the belief that everyone should be treated as an equal and as one wanted to be treated. He added that if the President needed any additional advice, he should come to the ranch for dinner and he would get an earful.

A day later Joe left to meet with the President.

President Lebak had spent the last several days thinking about the fact that Joe had asked for a private meeting to discuss how to handle finding a third human populated planet. He had spent the evening hours thinking through what it meant that there were three planets populated by human. He came to the conclusion that the history of Earth was about to be redefined. He was certain that the future would be a great challenge in how Earth would approach the fact that they were not the unique planet in the Universe. It was clear to him that Joe had that in mind and was most likely going to propose something that would deal with that situation. Whatever the reason, Joe had left his command and had returned to meet with him. He knew that every time he met with Joe he had a new challenge or a new financial bill. He smiled and figured he would soon know if again he would be given both a bill and a challenge by Joe. He walked into the room where he was announced to Five Star Admiral Joe Elsinger.

4 A Seed on Fertile Ground

When a short time later, he walked out of his meeting, he was a changed President. He had listened and had his fears about the interstellar human population confirmed. However, what really changed him was that Joe had proposed an organization that made so much sense that he not only was happy to fund it but wanted to be part of getting it established. He had agreed to having Rear Admirals Jorge Martinez and Jerald Delaney lead the establishment of the organization on the condition that he get to review and participate in its establishment. The change that he knew had taken place was that he had a new vision of how he wanted to conduct his next term as President. He wanted that term to focus on getting the world prepared for what by then most likely would be the introduction of the complete human family that was spread out across multiple galaxies. He wanted to be a key part of the growth of Earth and perhaps be the catalyst that brought peace across the entire planet.

Joe left the meeting relieved that the President had embraced the concept of the United Intergalactic Worlds Organization. He also liked the fact that extending the influence of his two Rear Admirals was accepted and the fact that the President had suggested several names of talented personnel that should be part of designing such an organization at the detailed levels that were most likely not in Jorge's or Jerry's background demonstrated to him that the President was giving not only the money to support the concept but putting boots on the ground that would ensure the idea had a successful beginning.

5

Return to the Quartet

I was fascinated by the visionary actions that the Admiral took as he looked ahead to finding the planets populated by humas that were scattered in a defined pattern across the Universe. He was envisioning how these planets might work together in a cooperative manner and how that cooperation would be facilitated if there was such an organization with a strong backbone and enforcement power. The backbone as he defined it was a fair structure that allowed each planet to manage their own affairs. The power was to have the capability to enforce the agreements made by the organization that was made up of members of all the worlds. He saw that enforcement capability to be the Cosmos Fleet that he commanded. He had no illusions that it would be the only force available but he was sure it was a force that would allow the United Intergalactic Worlds Organization to get its footing and establish itself. He hope not to need the enforcement arm but he was a realist and anticipated some worlds might have a different vision and different desires.

5 A Planet Awakens

It is interesting that the Admiral returned to Earth to test his ideas with his two Rear Admirals who he clearly described many times as his friends and mentors. He had become an Admiral but he saw the two as men who had earned his respect because they had spent years in the Airforce and in the Marine Corps and had earned their rank through service. He felt that he personally had skipped all the experience they had by being lucky enough to be in the right place at the right time. He did not want to bet and depend on luck. He wanted to plan strategically to ensure the outcome was what he wanted.

Rear Admiral Jorge Gonzalez documented his praise for the Admiral in great detail pointing out that true heroes never realize the impact that their actions have on the people around them and on the events that they personally guide to very specific and positive outcomes.

Rear Admiral Gerald Delaney adds to this that the Admiral was admired for his courage and for his willingness to put himself at the front as was the case when he was shot while protecting and saving the President from an assassin and taking the action that killed the assassin while blood ran from the wound that he had received. He pointed to numerous other events where the positive outcome was directly related to the Admirals actions.

As I read additional accounts of various exploits that the Admiral was involved in I too feel the presence of a person who should be thought of as a hero and a person who had indeed earned the right to be made a Five Star Admiral.

He was inspirational in almost every manner that I can think of. He elevated those that worked directly with him and he opened the door to all those that flowed into the support structures that he unwittingly caused to exist because of the very positive actions that he took.

I have studied many men and women in the histories of all nine human world planets and he by far stands out as a singularity. He is the rare individual that is humble, but who never hesitates to take positive action. He could never be accused of sitting on his hands. He by far was a catalyst of the most powerful kind. He changed the course of Humanity across the entire universe. The universe will wait a long time before another individual of his caliber and outstanding vision once again surfaces.

No one should worry about the light that illuminates his accomplishments dimming. His actions continue to expose a universe beyond what anyone ever imagined.

****

Joe returned from his jaunt to Earth and found everyone on the Cosmos Quartet awaiting him. The communication with the people on Gaja was now almost at a full conversational mode. He convened a four ship wide information sharing session and let everyone know that they were now officially on a journey that as they found each additional Human populated planet they would be enrolling them in The United Intergalactic Worlds Organization. This drew an enthusiastic "Voya…Voya…Voya" from everyone.

Lacey smiled and asked how President Lebak had taken the news that they were on track to finding multiple human populated worlds.

Joe replied that the President had sent his regards to her and joked that each visit to discuss the Cosmos effort seemed to cost him more.

Lacey laughed and said that his observation was true, but the return on investment would make him famous long after he was out of office. She asked if he had asked for a position in the Cosmos fleet.

Joe shook his head but did say that he had inquired about being part of the new United Intergalactic Worlds Organization.

Lacey nodded and said that he would be great at getting that organization up and on its feet and she added, "better he than me."

Kashanti spoke up and said that he and his team had put together a translation module that would allow simple conversations to occur with the people on Gaja and they wanted Joe to be the first to use it to do so.

Joe thanked him for the consideration and suggested that everyone gather in the back of the control room of each Cosmos ship, and he would introduce the eighty people that were a key and critical part of the venture.

Once the captains let him know that everyone was in place, he asked Kashanti to establish visual and audio communication with the Gajan contact. He said, "Hello, I am Joe Elsinger leader of the four groups of people you see in the picture. There are eighty of us on a journey of discovery. We are very pleased to have been able to find Gaja, the second planet we have visited, and our home planet Earth makes three planets of humans.

On Gaja, Zacker received the message and immediately conveyed it in its entirety to the leadership council. He was pleased that they wanted to send back a picture of the council members that consisted of one hundred and fifteen individuals almost equally divided between males and females. Zacker introduced the leader of the Council, Melidia Mecally who represented the largest city state.

Melidia came on and gave a slight bow and said that she was pleased to greet Joe and all the people that she saw on the screen. She went on to say that she hoped that they would be able to enjoy a long, positive, friendly, and close relationship.

Joe replied that he was also looking forward to a long and positive relationship. He stated that he and the people on screen were on a quest to find six more worlds that had humans on them.

Melidia nodded and said that legend on Gaja had it that their origin was out among the stars and that they were put on Gaja millions of years ago. She had always believed that was just an origin of life story but now she would have to rethink all her beliefs. She smiled and said that meeting other humans in such a friendly manner made doing so an event that she felt would enrich the people on Gaja.

Joe replied that reevaluating lifelong beliefs was what had happened to him and everyone around him. It was hard to overcome a lifetime and embrace a new reality. He added that the reality was that now he looked forward to learning about the Gaja history and the Gajan stories to see how they compared to the ones he had grown up with on Earth.

He was sure that such would be the case on all the worlds and in the end when all the chapters had been examined all their worlds would have matured and be at the top together.

He then said that he would be placing a module that was referred to as a Door that would house a small group of people that would establish a long term relationship with the people of Gaja.

He also hoped that once it was determined that Earthlings and Gajans were not a biological threat to each other the Gajans and all the other humans that were found could visit each other's planets and create an intergalactic family of humans.

Melidia replied that she and the council would look forward to the continued contact and that the Door module was of great interest because it was a concept that had been proposed by some of the Gajan scientists but it had been rejected for funding and now she wondered if those scientists had been on the right track. She added that it was a fascinating concept and the fact that it existed was hard to believe and it spoke to the power that Earth was able to demonstrate.

Joe replied that it was a new capability for Earth and it was transforming its society. He was sure that in the near future the Gajans would be able to utilize it and enjoy the fact the universe would be available to them. He closed by wishing the Gajan's well and welcomed them into the United Intergalactic Worlds Organization.

Once they were off line, Lydia asked Joe how that organization would function.

Joe shook his head and said that he hoped it would function similarly to the UN but he wanted it to have greater power by having an enforcement branch that was made up of the Cosmos ships.

Samantha asked if the President had bought into the enforcement part of the organization.

Joe nodded and replied that he was especially supportive since there might be some human populated planets that could be less than friendly.

He then explained that their two Rear Admirals were busy working with representatives that the President had identified to write the constitution for the United Intergalactic Worlds Constitution that would describe how the organization would be structured and how it would operate. He had suggested that it have the three branches of government: legislative, executive, and judicial similar to the current US constitution or at least it should include a system of checks and balances to prevent any one branch from becoming too powerful. It should also define the relationship between the worlds and the governing Intergalactic body. The United Intergalactic Worlds Constitution should establish the relationship between the worlds and the mechanism to enforce them. Finally, he had reminded them that it should include the process for amending the Constitution.

Yara asked how many people were working on the constitution and would the Cosmos team get a chance to input their ideas and evaluated the tone of the constitution.

H^3 added that the team out in the universe finding the planets should get a chance to influence the final product.

Darian seconded H^3's suggestion.

Joe nodded and asked Tom to gather the input from the team members and send the request back to Jorge and ask him to include all of them in the process of developing the constitution.

He then asked that the coordinates for the next planet be programed into the control system and that the Cosmos Quartet get prepared for the next planet.

6

The Fourth Colony

As I narrate the record of the discovery of the fourth very paranoid and aggressive human planet I am drawn by the unusual and surprising response that the Admiral had to the unfriendly, paranoid, aggressive reaction of the humans on that planet. He managed to bring the Cosmos Quartet through the Hole knowing that there was some sort of threat awaiting. He had the Quartet come through at full speed and to proceed directly toward the fourth Star in the random Ropa-a-Dope mode with orders not to respond to any aggressive actions that any of the ships might take. He ordered that the planets with intelligent life be identified as rapidly as possible.

It is recorded that as soon as the fourth planet was identified as the populated planet he ordered the Cosmos Quartet to fly directly towards it. Three ships similar to any individual Cosmos ship were chasing the Quartet trying to stop it. The record shows that the chasing ships were no match in speed or armament. The Admiral had the Quartet send his picture with his empty hand as a gesture of friendship but at the same time he ordered the launch of a missile and had it explode well away from the planet but clearly indicating that he could hit it at will.

6 The Fourth Colony

The records show that he then had the Quartet stop and await the response. It highlights that as he waited for a response the three chasing ships approached and took several shots at the him. His response was to launch three space Tomahawk missiles and explode them in front of the three but far enough away that there would be no damage to the ships. There is speculation that he had his laser operators paint their lasers around the rotating shells of the alien human ships and the response was that the ships that had been in pursuit blinked their exterior lights on and off. It surprised me as I dug deeper into the record that the sweep of the lasers was to determine if there was a shield that might protect the three ships. The sweep verified that the three ships did not have any shielding similar to that surrounding the Quartet. Their response also clearly indicated that they recognized the ease with which the Quartet could destroy the three ships. It was good that the three signaled that they were ceasing their aggressive attack.

The response to the raised hand picture came in from one of the cities on the planet and it had a similar picture of a person with an open empty hand in the air. This was the beginning of a long series of communications to establish a working relationship.

He had Kashanti try to improve their communication with the people on the Fourth planet so they could learn the basic information as they had done with the Gajans.

Records show that during the wait, Tom and H^3 were scouring the planet to identify the major population centers. They did and had them all categorized as to what they had determined were their capabilities.

Captain Lydia Tabata had her personnel scrutinizing the three spaceships design and armament. They reported that the ships were of similar design to the four Cosmos ships, rotated fast enough to create slightly higher than a one G of force and they were slightly smaller and less heavily armed. If this was an accurate record, it clearly showed how lucky the three ships were to have faced someone as restrained in his actions as the Admiral.

****

Joe had to restrain himself as he waited for everything to get set up with the Gajans. It took several weeks that allowed those that wanted to take R&R back on Earth to do so. Joe had worked with the Captains to establish a staffing level that allowed a certain percentage of the personnel to rotate to Earth on R&R. The realization that it was relatively easy to do so meant that going on leave from the Quartet was no different than applying and taking leave back on Earth. This added a sense of normality to the journey they were on.

Joe also spent time thinking through how he would handle meeting the humans that might not be as friendly as the Gajans and might have more powerful weapons or faster spaceships. He worried about meeting humans that existed on a world that more closely mirrored the behaviors and attitudes of that Earth might have to any strange spaceships appearing in the region around Earth. He discussed the situation with the rest of his team.

6 The Fourth Colony

Linda was the one that commented that one either chose not to fight or needed to put on a superior display of power so that the humans that were at the aggressive end of the spectrum would get the message they would lose the confrontation.

Darian agreed and said that their shields gave them the ability to withstand a significant number of hits but they should not dismiss the fact that there might be a force that would penetrated their shields.

Joe had listened as the various viewpoints were shared. He then said that he wanted to make sure that the transit through the Hole was one that provided them a means of exiting in such a manner that they were not sitting a sitting duck waiting to be hit with a missile or laser barrage. He asked that both the cleaning lasers and the defense lasers have cameras mounted on them so the Cosmos Quartet would have eyes on the other side of the hole and knew what to expect as it went through the hole. He also wanted to change the way they came out into the clean zone.

He reminded everyone that the cleaning of the area was done to prevent the dust particles in the transit end point from ending up in their bodies. However, he made the point that there was no need to stop at the specific Hole termination coordinates. They could come through at full speed and continue flying through that area. In fact, they could assume a random twisting flight pattern until they could locate any threats. To be able to do this the lasers would need to move aside so that they would be out of the way.

He then declared that for the next transit the Cosmos Quartet would go through the Hole at full speed and assume a random flight pattern and if being attacked go into the Ropa-a-Dope mode of flying through space. If attacked they would locate their attackers and decide how to respond based on the number of attackers and the attackers response to a sign of friendship.

He asked that Tom, H^3 and Darian assume the role of determining the coordinates of any attackers and the coordinates of the planet that had the intelligent life on it.

Tom said that he would focus on identifying the planet.

H^3 said he would focus on identifying the location of any attacker.

Darian volunteered to assess the attackers armament capabilities.

Joe thanked everyone for their participation and announced that in two days they would transit through the next Hole. He cancelled all leave and gave a time when everyone was to be on board the Quartet. He followed up with Linda to ensure that the coordinates for the next solar system where the fourth human colony was located were entered into the Hole generation cannon control system.

He assigned Yara to be the one to take them through the hole at full speed and continue on into a random flight path. He asked the other three captains to be the spotters to determine how close any munitions exploded as they flew through space. He wanted them to determine when they would reply with a display of power, but they should position their display in such a manner that the attacking humans would not lose their ships or their lives.

He described how he wanted to display their power. He wanted Tomahawk explosions to the left and right of the oncoming of the ship or ships to rock them. He then wanted to follow up with one in front of the ships that again would be felt by the ship or ships. He added that the warnings were similar to what ships at sea did to warn those they were going into battle when the battle was not desired by the ship giving the warning.

Samantha asked what the next step would be if the attack continued.

Joe nodded and said that his technique would be to shoot them in the leg. He would order the laser operators to take out the engines that provided the forward acceleration of the ship if that was the case.

A day later, Lacey announced that all her personnel were back except one Sparrow operator who had called in to let her know that she was to be in court because of a car accident. She had given that operator conditional leave to attend court and ordered her to return afterwards. She had also requested that Jorge assign a lawyer to represent her in court.

Joe nodded and said that she should assign the position to someone in case they were in an all-out battle.

He was pleased with the response to his cancelling R&R and the return of all those on leave. It was really a great sign of how the crew felt about their assignment to the Cosmos ships.

Esoteric Journey

The atmosphere on all four ships was of a close community. There was ship to ship interactions and relations across the ships. He was aware of a chess club that had the name Cosmos Knights, a Violin trio that was called the Cosmos Three and a String Quartet that called themselves the Cosmos Quartetto. There was a history class that had the a goal of digging into the history of each of the nine human populated planets that had named itself Historic Roots of Cosmic Humanity.

He was especially impressed that the four Cosmos Captains had organized an art class that focused on painting scenes of the planets that had intelligent life on them and had called the class the Unleashed Cosmos Strokes. The Captains had each painted a scene of what had captured their imagination and it seemed that Lacey painted in the Realism style whereas Yara was into pop art, Samantha was challenging them with digital art and Lydia had more of a Romanticist style. He personally was participating in their art class and had focused on imaginative optical abstraction. The art was displayed along the walkways that went around each of the wheels. Each of the musical groups would hold performances along the walkways as well. The historical club provided a digital interface to the work they were doing. The Cosmos Quartet community was an example on a small scale that he envisioned on the grand scale of the Universe.

6 The Fourth Colony

The day for the next transit arrived. The Cosmos Odessey II was the ship in control of the Hole generation and the transit. Joe was sitting behind Yara as she commanded the Hole operator to create the Hole. As soon as the cleaning lasers and the protection lasers completed their work Yara noted that all the lasers had turned in one direction and were blinking red. The lasers recorded three different objects in their sights and gave the exact coordinates of the objects. The camera's that had been mounted on the lasers provided the surprise when the objects they were pointed at were three ships that were almost duplicates of a single rotating Cosmos ship.

Yara gave the order to send the Cosmos Quatro through at full speed with the Odyssey II facing the three vessels. She immediately gave the order to go into the Rope-a-dope behavior as they entered into the random flight pattern.

The ships of the fourth planet led by Endilo had moved their ships out towards the sphere of lasers that for some mysterious reason seemed to be shooting inwards but as they approached all the lasers in the rather large sphere in space turned and aimed at them.

The lasers had appeared from nowhere. He gave the order to halt and to wait and see what else would happen. He had all weapons active and ready to use should any of the lasers fire. He then witnessed a sphere appear as if materializing magically and speeding out from the center of the sphere made by the lasers pointed at him.

He ordered all ships weapons to fire on the sphere that seemed to be out of control and flying randomly toward the sixth planet, Aggla, which was a primary supplier of the minerals critical for the industries on his planet, Edalia. He then gave the order to intercept the sphere and to destroy what appeared to be a threat to their solar system. He looked out to the bright orange star that was his home and made a wish on Iliady that he would successfully destroy the alien invaders.

His communications leader let him know that there was a very disturbing message that displayed a person that looked almost like any Edalian with an empty hand raised in the air in the sign of friendship.

Endilo laughed when he saw the picture and said that he was impressed that the aliens had done their homework and knew what an Edalian looked like, but he was not going to be fooled by such trickery. He ordered a round of missiles to blow the aliens out of space.

The random nature of the sphere's flight seemed to be giving his three ships a problem of keeping up. He had watched several of his missiles hit the sphere with no discernible damage. He was surprised at the fact that the sphere appeared rather fragile but that it could withstand the force of one of his missiles.

Suddenly he realized that what seemed to be a random flight path was now heading directly toward Edalia and his ships were not able to close in on it.

He was about to order another round of missiles to be launched when an explosion on his left knocked wheel one toward his ship then an explosion on the right knocked wheel three toward his ship and suddenly an explosion directly in front of wheel two caused it to almost stop. He was sure he would have bruises from the force that his harness had exerted to keep him in his command chair. He understood the message and ordered his ships to cease pursuit.

He noted that the alien sphere also stopped. It was then that he noticed that the part of the sphere facing him was rotating exactly as his ship did. He was more than surprised when his science officer let him know that the spinning of that part of the sphere almost exactly matched the radial spinning force of his ship.

Once again his communications leader said that a second picture, this time of a female holding her hand up showing an empty hand had been received.

This time he decided to send back a reply with his hand raised to see what would happen. A moment later the picture with a male holding his open hand up was returned. He decided that it was time to get his countries elected leaders involved in communicating with a group that appeared to be people from Edalia. He wondered which country had been able to develop such technology to make the sphere.

By this time, he had been informed that the sphere was comprised of four ships of similar design to his own. It seemed to him that surprises were hitting him faster than he could absorb and comprehend them.

He was informed that each of his three ships had been painted with a weak laser that seemed to be teasing them to take action. He was also informed that the missiles that had exploded around them were at least one hundred times more powerful than any missile they had on their ships and possibly any that Edalia had as land based missiles.

He was amazed. It seemed that the power of the sphere floating in front of him was something out of one of his nightmares. All that he could think about was that even if he sacrificed his three ships the sphere would remain intact.

On the Quartet, Tom had been frantically gathering the data on the inhabited planet.

Lydia had verified that the three ships did not have any shielding. They were slightly smaller than any of the Cosmos ships but were generating about a one G gravitational force.

Tom added that matched what the force of gravity was on the fourth planet. He added that there seemed to be trade or at least industry like mining being done on planets four and five. The slightly Orange sun was providing a wide goldilocks zone for the three planets.

Kashanti said that he was now receiving a message from the planet with a person with their open hand raised and a picture of the Quartet Sphere and what he took to be a question mark but that was his own take on the picture.

6 The Fourth Colony

Joe asked Kashanti to reply with the picture of the Quartet supper imposed on his open hand picture. That picture was to be followed up with the picture of Earth and the sun, a picture of Nivian and their sun, a picture of Gaja and their sun and it should end with a picture of the fourth planet and its sun. Once Kashanti let him know that the pictures had been sent Joe decided to wait.

Endilo was following the communications between the Edalian leaders and the beings on the sphere. His personal world was flipped on its head as the meaning of the pictures penetrated his mind. The narrative that he had always been taught that he thought was fictional about a superior race seeding his planet seemed to be coming true. He wondered if the people on the sphere were the seeders of Edalia.

The exchange of messages took on the tone of a student asking the teacher to give him information. They showed Iliady and all the planets and seemed to be asking for names. They then showed the male and gave what appeared to be labels to the different parts. It became clear to Endilo that the beings were trying to establish the basis to establish meaningful communications.

His radar specialist let him know that all of the lasers that had created the sphere where the ship had first appeared were all homing in on where they were now located. They were grouped together and their lasers were pointing down.

Endilo looked at the video. He knew that he was not going to do anything about the situation but watch. The ability to retrieve the lasers in such a manner was a display of technical capability that surpassed any that Edalia currently was capable of.

He followed the retrieval process and watched as each laser positioned itself and was then pulled in at the center of the rotating wheel facing his three ships.

Joe realized that setting up the communications would take some time. He ordered everyone to stand down and to rotate to the mess or go on break.

Tom had been busy scrutinizing the planet which seemed to be called Edalia. He commented that it was a very industrial planet that had three separate continents that were surrounded by water. It seemed that the other two planets in the Golkdiloc zone were being mined or used to produce food for planet four. Planet four seemed to have one government for each continent.

They were communicating with the leaders of the largest continent which seemed to control the three ships that were facing them.

Joe thanked him for the information and said that he was going to go back to the Voyager and he was turning over command of the Quartet to Yara. He wanted to be reengaged when they got past the learn to speak mode and were getting into the embrace each other mode.

6 The Fourth Colony

7

The Fifth Planet

After the surprise attack as they crossed over through the Hole to the Fourth human planet, it is recorded that the Admiral modified the cross over preparation process. He chose to eliminate the group of protection lasers and rely solely on the dust clearance lasers. He had them modified so that once they stopped removing the fine dust particles they automatically adopted the role of a defense perimeter, provided visual information and when ordered fired at any attacker. He wanted the Cosmos Quartet to come through ready to fire warning shots and do so as they went into their evasive maneuvers. He stayed in the Iliady solar system while the communication was enhanced to the point that the leaders on the planet understood that the Door module was a means of housing the translation and negotiating team and that the module had significant self-defense capability. The Admiral had the new Door modules that were shielded and had a Sparrow system mounted on it. It is recorded that his attitude about keeping his people safe had hardened based on his experiences.

My studies show that it was not so much being hardened but of applying the ranch life experiences that had molded him. He was said to have commented that even a docile milk cow would kick her milk bucket if she was frightened. I believe he extended that saying into how frightened humans seemed to react to high level of tension, risk, or uncertainty, the unexpected and at the tipping point for social beliefs. He is quoted as saying that the appearance of an alien vessel inferred that the outcome could have significant negative consequences and made the meeting particularly tense and potentially dangerous triggering the human flee or fight response or an otherwards "they kicked the bucket."

I have studied the modifications to the through the Hole process and determined that it provided a fifty percent faster through the Hole transit and the modification of the cleaning laser's actions and self-defense actions improved the statistics of survival by more than one hundred percent. I also learned that some of the changes that came about were discussed informally during a trip of the Admiral to the ranch with his two Rear Admirals. It is said that the three went fishing and during that time they also discussed how the United Intergalactic Worlds Organization establishment was progressing. It is interesting how the Admiral mixed his personal life with his exploration of the universe. It is clear to me that he was a very unassuming but unusual person.

Esoteric Journey

The timing of the through the Hole procedural change was fortuitous because the transition through the Hole to the solar system of the fifth human seeded planet was met by an attack from a very powerful ship that had technology that was unknown to Earth and a ship that was faster than the Cosmos Quartet. The breakthrough technology of the fifth planet was later documented to be the invention of a gravity generator and of rocket engines that converted water into hydrogen and oxygen that when alternately exploded gave the turbine like engines power that surpassed those on the Cosmos Quartet.

The Admiral admitted that his communications team was able to hack into the computer systems on the planet and steal the plans for both technologies. He later arranged to have the fifth human colony reimbursed for that technology but he went on to give that technology credit for his ability to improve the Cosmos Quartet in such a manner that made it faster and more fuel efficient because he no longer needed fuel to keep the wheels rotating to generate a gravity like force. He also pointed out that the new modernized Cosmos ships would take on the more traditional look of the early space rocket designs that were less expensive to build and the building could be done on the ground.

As soon as the technology was in his hands the Admiral made a journey back to Earth to get it into Rear Admiral Delaney's hands with orders to build the first Cosmos Rocket with built in three hundred and sixty degree gravity. The request for three hundred and sixty degree gravity was an invention that clearly came from the Admiral's own imagination.

As always I was mesmerized as I documented the Admiral's achievements and visionary ideas.

****

Joe had patiently waited for the process of establishing a working relationship with the people of Edalia to propagate on its own. He chose to take leave and return to the ranch. This time he convinced Lydia to take leave at the same time. The two to them were met by Jorge and Jerry at the Door building in the wee hours of the new day. The sun had yet to break the horizon and Jorge suggested that they have an early breakfast.

Lydia shook her head and suggested that they all get on the hilo and go to the ranch. Once there they could all relax, have breakfast, exchange any formal information that made sense and then decide between doing some fishing or riding the range.

Jorge smiled and said that he was all for it. He only wanted to get out of his uniform and into some ranch clothes.

Jerry nodded and said that he too wanted to get appropriately dressed to go fishing.

Lydia and Joe took a car to the hilo area where they were greeted by Tyler and Veetry who were all smiles as they helped the two on board. The two of them added that thanks to the very early hour they had been able to get the assignment to fly the two of them without it costing them an arm and a leg.

Lydia nodded and said that once again their perseverance was going to pay off if they could stay for breakfast.

Veetry nodded and said that they both would love to sit at Uncle Ted's table and eat whatever was for breakfast.

About the time that they ended the introduction banter, Jorge and Jerry arrived and got into the hilo.

Joe complemented them on looking like all the hired hands on the ranch.

The ride out allowed Joe to describe the interaction and battle with the three vessels that were virtual duplicates of the Cosmos ships. They were slower and smaller and lacked the armament or the shielding that the Cosmos ships had but otherwise they could have been built on Earth. He shared the fact that the interaction they had with the ships of the fourth colony had made him change the procedure of transiting through the Hole. He went on to describe the change and asked if either Jorge or Jerry had any suggestions.

Jerry suggested that the laser power should be reduced to give whatever it hit a kick but is should not tear it apart. This would allow for the lasers to distract any attackers but do minimal damage.

Joe nodded and replied that he would have that change arranged.

7 The Fifth Planet

Jorge asked if there was a way to get the speed through the hole boosted. He suggested anchoring six of the Tomahawk missiles and firing them as the Cosmos Quartet went through the hole to give the entire structure a significant boost in the speed coming through the hole.

Joe replied that he would implement that idea.

Their arrival at the Ranch ended the conversation but the ideas that had been shared were ones that Joe knew would make a difference in how they would transit through the next hole. He put that thought aside as they got out of the hilo and were greeted by Uncle Ted and his father.

After breakfast, the hilo pilots left and Joe led the way down to the creek to do some fishing. He continued his conversation with Jorge about how getting the United Intergalactic Worlds Organization organized and functioning was progressing.

Jorge shared that getting the organization established was well underway. He had chosen to recruit representatives from each of the planets that had so far been discovered. That connection seemed to be a fruitful one that seemed to be embraced by the two planets and each had set up a team to review and input to the charter that they were developing.

The fishing picked up and everyone focused on the fishing with a periodic side bar about what was happening with the Cosmos ships that were focused on establishing the Nivian planet infrastructure and getting the migration of the Nivians to the planet flowing at full speed.

After catching enough fish for a good lunch Joe suggested they clean the fish and turn them over to Uncle Ted and get him to prepare lunch.

Lydia had chosen not to go fishing knowing that much of the conversation would be linked with the activities associated with the human planets they were discovering. Instead, she walked the tree line discussing the ranch activities and the politics of the country with Trey. She learned that the other countries in the world were slowly understanding that the US had a tremendous lead that no longer was thought of as a space race but had taken on the characteristic features of the behavior that had permeated the world during the "The Age of Imperialism" and again during the "Scramble for Africa." Trey added that the other countries wanted a piece of the action but had no leverage to get what they wanted. Lydia had listened to Trey's explanation and closed the topic by saying that given the fact that Joe was successfully leading them in discovering the nine human planets that the team agreed were spread across the universe and establishing an organization that would represent each planet, the other countries on Earth would need to consider participating as contributors and not as colonist nations.

Uncle Ted turned the fish into the lunch center piece surrounded by grilled asparagus, grill potato slices and a tossed tomato, chopped onion and cucumber salad.

7 The Fifth Planet

After lunch Jorge and Jerry bade adios and took a hilo back to Lakland.

Lydia and Joe had agreed on a ride across the ranch and a stop at their favorite swim hole. They planned to stay the night and go back to their ship in the morning.

The next day upon his return to the Cosmos Voyager, Joe gave a day's notice to the opening of the next Hole.

He spent the day working with Tom and H^3 on the coordinates for the Hole.

He worked with Samantha on the way she should bring the Cosmos Quartet through the hole.

Samantha said she liked using the Tomahawk missiles to give the Cosmos Quartet extra speed as they went through the Hole.

He commented that it seemed that they must be finding the planets in reverse order to when they had been seeded because it seemed that each time they were stepping up in the level of technology that they were encountering. He commented that the break throughs that Tom and Linda had given Earth by creating the Door and then creating the Hole generator had put Earth a step ahead of the planets that they had so far visited. They had encountered a non-human race that had invented the shield that was significantly more advanced than anything that Earth had, so he was aware that there were civilizations that had greater capabilities. He figured that they might run into human populations that also had more advanced technology than Earth and they needed to be ready for that situation.

Samantha agreed that it seemed that they were going around the base in the reverse order of the establishment of each human populated planet. She wondered if Earth had been the last to be seeded.

Joe nodded and said that he believed that was the case. They were the last but they probably were the first to figure out that there were eight seeded planets and a ninth seeding planet. It was clear that Earth was the only planet that was looking for the other seeded planets.

Joe always chose to take the journey through the Hole in the morning time. He felt this had the crew fresh and ready for whatever they found on the other side of the Hole.

Samantha gave the order to generate the Hole and immediately sent the cleaning lasers through. They watched as the cleaning lasers finished doing their job and several of them were hit by small missile fire. She had the remaining lasers turn toward the where the missiles had originated and had them fire just short of the target. She ordered the Quartet to go through at maximum speed and had the anchored Tomahawk missiles providing the extra boost of speed. She had the random flight pattern programed and entered it as soon as she crossed through. The Quartet went through the sphere region with several explosions going off behind them.

7 The Fifth Planet

Commander Rately was alerted to the objects that appeared and positioned themselves in a large sphere and began to fire some sort of weapon around the sphere that had been formed. He took it to be a display of some sort of weapon that he was unfamiliar with. He decided to see if his missiles were effective in destroying what appeared to be automated weapons. He had destroyed two of the alien weapons when suddenly a sphere of some sort appeared and proceeded to fly out of the circle in a random flight pattern. He had a missile launched to see if it would have the ability to disable the sphere. It was clear that his missiles had been too slow in reaching the sphere. He hesitated for a moment when a missile exploded immediately in front of his ship.

He contemplated his next move and decided that he would pursue the alien vessel. He was pleased that at top speed he was closing in on the sphere but he also learned that the missiles he had fired were either not hitting or when they did hit seemed to have no effect. He had his crew trying to determine if the alien ship had any significant armament when suddenly a missile of some sort was fired from the weaving and randomly flying sphere and exploded close enough that the explosion caused his rocket to veer to his left. Then another missile exploded and caused his vessel to veer to his right. Then suddenly one exploded directly in front of him and he realized that the aliens had the capability and the power to destroy his ship but had instead warned him by expertly placing their missile explosions around him. He heeded their warning and stopped the chase.

He was wondering what the next move on the aliens part would be when his communication officer let him know that he had received a message from the aliens, but he was confused because the video of the alien looked very much like anyone of the ship's crew.

Samantha had sent out the now standard picture of Joe holding up his empty hand and was waiting for a reply before having Kashanti take over the communication. She was pleased that her shot over the bow of the approaching and very fast spaceship had caused it to stop and allow the communication to take place.

H^3 was busily trying to hack into the control system on the ship that they were communicating with. He and one of the communications technicians had combined their talents to see if they could hack into the computer network that they had probed and been able to get into. They were surprised that there was no firewall. It was the first time in her life that the tech had experienced a computer system with no firewall. She went crazy digging into the records that were available to her. She did a huge dump of the content that was stored in the computers on the ship and put it all on one of the crystal memory cubes for later analysis. She extended her hacking and was able to get into computers that were remotely located somewhere on the planet. She was not sure what planet but she was sure that she had unfettered access to everything.

7 The Fifth Planet

Linda and Tom began going over the material in the memory cube and together they interpreted drawings that described the gravity generator that the ship from the fifth planet had. The mathematics and the design were not that difficult once they had set their goal to decipher the drawings that they printed out and poured over. Linda recognized the point where the gravitation generator created the gravity. She shared this with Joe who asked if the gravity generators could be placed under the spinning walkways. She nodded and said that they had the materials on hand to make at least one set of gravity generators and they could figure out how to mount the units.

Joe asked her to do so and if it worked he would schedule a trip back to Earth to share their find with Jerry and get him to build a new version of a Cosmos ship that would be more efficient than the current spinning wheel design. He asked if the force of gravity could be radial so that the walkways in a rocket could be layered along the outer walls of a rocket shaped vessel.

Linda answered that she, Tom and H^3 would work on that concept. She agreed that it would make the interior of a rocket shaped vessel very effective and the living conditions greatly enhanced.

Joe turned his attention to the communication that was underway with the people on the Spaceship.

Linda, Tom and H^3 continued pouring over the drawings and realized that they had the drawings for the engines that were noticeably more powerful than any that they were aware of.

They worked on developing their understanding and realized that the concept had been pursued on Earth. It was a pulsing explosion design that had been abandoned. They did not know why it had been abandoned but the fact that it was a fully developed and powerful engine on the space ship facing them made them think that someone on Earth had dropped the ball. They were sure that they would be able to guide Jerry's engineering team in creating the engines. The three of them celebrated that fact that they were going to be able to create another discontinuity in the Cosmos program.

Once the communication with the fourth planet was well underway and the people on the planet had accepted having a Door module orbiting their planet, Joe decided that he would take the Cosmos Quartet back to Earth and have the gravity generators installed in all the Cosmos ships.

Linda had let him know about the engine design so he added that to the improvements that he wanted to put on all the Cosmos ships. He also had decided that if gravity could be added to a rocket like shape then the wheel design of the Cosmos ships should be abandoned and eventually all ships would have a missile like shape. This meant that the entire construction process could be done on the surface and working out in space would not be required.

He shared his vision of a revamped Cosmos fleet with all the Cosmos Captains and got resounding support. He was sure that he would get the same support from President Lebak though he would complain about the cost.

7 The Fifth Planet

Commander Rately had his team monitoring the sphere. They reported that there were four modules that were spinning. They speculated that the spin provided the equivalent of gravity that was equal to the gravity on Witmeia. He correctly speculated that the beings had not developed the gravity generator.

He was very curious when they placed the cubicle module in orbit around Witmeia. An initial scan indicated it was empty, then a later scan indicated that there were several beings occupying it. There had been no physical travel to the module. He wondered how the beings had gained access to the module. He was also informed that the module appeared to be armed with weapons of an unknown design. He realized that he was experiencing several technologies that were unknown to he and the people of Witmeia.

Clearly he was facing an advanced version of Witmeans and he wondered why they had not discovered how to generate gravity. It was clear that the beings had weapons that were significantly more powerful than what he had or that Witmeia had down on the planet. It was also very clear to him that the beings had demonstrate their superior fire power but had refrained from responding to the attack that he now felt had been ill advised but that had been ordered by the ground control center. He wanted to thank the person in command of the Sphere for the restrained response to his attack. He felt it spoke highly of the attitude of whomever was in command of the sphere.

Rately ended his speculation when he watched the sphere fly to its point of origin retrieve the weapons that had preceded it and then suddenly vanish. In the future he would need to find out how that could possibly be.

7 The Fifth Planet

8

Technology Assimilation

The record of the journey around the eight planets that is referred to as the base of an eight pointed polygon. When the apex it considered it becomes a pyramid with eight sides. It clearly is an unusual shape that the Admiral and his team had identified. They were traveling around the base to discover the planets that had been seeded with humans.

The Admiral is on record admitting that he did not shy away from leveraging the technology possessed by each of the seeded planets or any other alien. The shields that the Cosmos ships utilized was reverse engineered from alien technology. He openly admits assimilating the gravitation and the nuclear fission pulsed plasma rocket engine technology that his team was able to obtain surreptitiously from the humans on the fourth planet. These engines were more efficient than any of the engines on his Cosmos ships and were capable of generating speeds that were significantly higher than the Cosmos ships had ever achieved. He immediately integrated those technologies.

8 Technology Assimilation

My studies show that he returned to Earth before proceeding to the location of the fifth planet. It shows that the stay was brief but upon departure the wheels were no longer spinning because the gravitational field generators had been put on the four ships that composed the Cosmos Quartet. The pulsed engines were not yet available because of the complexity of getting them fabricated but all the rockets that had provided the wheel rotational power were now harnessed to provide additional speed. In fact, it is recorded that the additional rockets increased the speed of the Cosmos Quartet by forty percent.

As always the Admiral visited the ranch, rode his horse Yin, and was accompanied by his wife Lydia on her horse Yang. I was fascinated by the names of their horses and laughed when I learned that Yin and Yang are complementary opposites but they are interdependent and strive for balance, meaning that neither could exist without the other, and their interaction created harmony through their contrasting energies. This seemed to describe the solid equilibrium the Admiral and Lydia enjoyed is recorded to have. I was jealous of such a relationship. I personally had not so far found the person that I would have such a relationship with.

Records also show that he met with then President Lebak and shared the breakthrough in the ability to generate gravity and the realization that the development of the pulsed rocket engine that the US abandoned was one that the humans on the latest planet had developed.

Esoteric Journey

It is said that the President hung his head and said that if he kept spending money on the Cosmos Program he would risk his successor being from the opposite party. What I am impressed with was that the Admiral agreed but said that he had a role that an ex-President could have in the Cosmos Program that would counter any negative action that the opposite party might take.

I was curious what such a role might have been. When I studied what the President did after his term in office ended I learned that he was given the Rank of Admiral in the Cosmos program with the responsibility of collecting dues from every world that was a member of the United Intergalactic Worlds Organization. It turned out that the President was an excellent fund raiser and the Cosmos program became totally funded by that organization.

It is fascinating that the two Presidents that had elevated the Admiral to the rank of Five Star Admiral benefited by his actions on their behalf.

It is also recorded that Rear Admiral Delaney was able to leverage both technologies that the Admiral had brought back and expedited the construction of the first missile shaped spaceship that incorporated the new technologies. When the next planet was visited he was able to send out an emissary offering to replace the Cosmos Quartet with a ship that had the space for all four crews, had gravity, had the shield technology and had engines that would provide a speed that would be unmatched by any vessel that had traveled space up to that point.

I am amazed that the records just could not bring out the dynamic nature of what the Admiral was capable of achieving.

8 Technology Assimilation

****

Joe's unannounced return with the Cosmos Quartet surprised the control center personnel. Visual inspection of the ships making up the Sphere showed some slight damage but nothing significant enough to cause alarm. Jorge looked at the Sphere and when he heard Hola, cómo estás, all is fine with us and we have a surprise, he smiled and replied Hablemos durante la cena en mi casa, let's talk over dinner at my place, he repeated in English so he would not confuse any of the techs in the control center. He correctly figured that Joe would only be returning if he wanted something that needed his or Jerry's attention.

Joe enjoyed the banter that had been initiated by Lydia upon their re-entry into orbit around Earth. He accepted the invitation to dinner and figured that he would make his request of getting the gravity generators expedited in hopes of having them for the next segment of the journey. He had no expectations that the pulsed engines could be built in the short time he planned to be in orbit around Earth.

He announced a two week window where all leaves would be granted.

Lydia put her second in charge and headed to the Door room where Joe was waiting. Once he had transited to Earth she followed. She smiled as she entered their dressing room and noticed that the white Admiral' suit hung untouched and Joe was buckling up his inch and half wide belt with his favorite brass buckle.

He smiled and said that after which ever meal they would be eating with Jorge, he planned to make a B-line to the Ranch. She nodded and said that she would be out shortly and opened her locker.

Joe walked out and was greeted by both Jorge and Jerry who were in their full Rear Admiral uniforms. He complemented them on looking great in them and tossed the information cube to Jerry as he said, "Rear Admiral Delaney that information cube has the top technologies that Tom and my top computer hacker was able to get from the computers of the latest humans that we encountered. Your job is to build the gravity generator and the nuclear pulse engine that are supposedly recorded on that cube." He then smiled, said that their official meeting was over, looked at Jorge and asked which meal of the day he had arrived for.

Jorge gave Joe a salute and then came over and gave him a hug and welcome him for to lunch. He suggested that they get a meeting room at the Cosmos club and do lunch there. He would also arrange for the hilo to take him to the ranch afterwards.

Lydia came out to the three gave a salute and then proceeded to give each of them hugs. She looked up at the clear cloudless sky, smiled and said that she guessed they were in time for lunch. She added that it seemed hot enough that she figured it must be July.

Jorge nodded and said that she was right on all counts and congratulated her on being able to keep track of time while traversing across the universe.

When they got to the club, Jerry gave the cube to the driver and told him to take it to the office and deliver it to the technical team with instruction for them to dig into the secrets it held.

At lunch Joe spent the time before the meal's arrival sharing how the modified entry process had saved them from direct hits by an attacking spaceship that was shaped like a very large but standard rocket shape. He added that Tom later learned that the rocket had gravity. He and one of the young female technicians who was an excellent hacker were able to get into the ships and later computers on the planet and get the engineering drawings that detailed how the gravity generators were constructed as well as the plans for the nuclear blast engines that gave the ship a much greater speed than the Cosmos ships had.

Joe smiled and said that he was assuming the role of Wimpy in the Popeye cartoons who always said, "I'll gladly pay you Tuesday for a hamburger today," only in this case, "Earth will gladly pay Witneia in the future for gravity and pulse engines in the future for the technology today, applied.

Jerry laughed, looked at Jorge, told him he should focus on being an Rear Admiral then asked how fast Joe wanted the technology.

Joe leaned toward him and said that he would love to have the gravity technology before he took the Cosmos Quartet on to the fifth planet and he would love to have a Cosmos Rocket with radial gravity on it and also have the pulse engines built by the time he returned from the fifth planet visit.

Jerry nodded and said that as always money would talk the loudest.

Joe looked over Jorge and asked him to arrange a meeting with the President and he would meet with him to see if he could squeeze a few more billion dollars from the current budget and have it moved into the Cosmos program budget.

Jorge nodded and asked if when Joe had gone through the Door the first time he had ever thought that his future would have him going throughout the universe to discover other human worlds.

Joe smiled and said that the only thing he was thinking about on his first trip through the Door was that Lydia was on the other side.

Lunch was delivered as Lydia leaned over and gave Joe a kiss on his cheek. She too knew that the two of them had become soul mates when both of them had been cured of their cancers by being two of the first three humans to transit through the Door.

During lunch Jerry got a call and excused himself and went to the corner of the private room they were in. He didn't have much to say because he was listening to his technical team who were animatedly and excitedly sharing what they were getting from the information cube. They were explaining that the gravity generator was physically similar to how a motor coil was wound but had a specific weave pattern and a control system that regulated the current flow through each coil wrapping that then generated a magnetic field that radiated outward from the coil to provide gravity.

They all were in agreement that something so simple should have already been discovered. They also said that since there were no moving parts they would have a lab version up and running the following day and they could meet the time line of installing gravity on the ships that made up the Quartet.

He then learned that the pulsed engine was more complicated but Earth had a similar engine that had been built by one of the top aircraft manufacturers but discontinued because they could not get the reliability up and the funding hat run out. They highlighted subtle but significant differences and the fact that the engine was powered by a nuclear core which gave it limitless fuel. The engines would require periodic maintenance to replace the explosion chambers that would slowly be eroded by the pulsing explosion process. They added that if the engines were on a rocket that could land on Earth, maintenance of the engines could be handled similarly to that done on jet plane engines.

Jerry returned to the table and said that Joe had once again enthralled his engineering team who were very excited about the technology. He added that it would take about a month for gravity to be available on the Quartet.

Lydia let out a low whistle and said that she would have to see how that changed how the current Cosmos ship would be handled. She thought it would have little to no effect but she was sure that there would be a degree of added stability.

Jerry then said that a space ship with gravity and the engines might be possible within a year if he could get one of the private rocket companies to sell them a massive rocket that they had been struggling to make functional. The company was having trouble with its current engine design and had several test engines experience massive explosions. He figured if he had that rocket shell that he would hollow out to make the interior of a spaceship and had the engines and gravity generators he would be able to have it converted in that period of time.

Joe nodded and said that the meeting with the President was a crucial step so Jerry would have the money to finance the rocket.

Jorge smiled and said that he would make sure Joe had that meeting.

After lunch Joe and Lydia headed out to the hilo pad where they met up with Tyler and Veetry and got on the way to the Ranch.

8 Technology Assimilation

9

Focused Political Message

The many attempts to assassinate the Admiral is well documented. It amazes me that there were individuals willing to bankroll assassination attempts against an individual like the Admiral that was opening the heavens to the people on Earth. The attacks more or less seemed to escalate over time. I focus this account on a missile attack on the Admiral, that was very close to a success but ended very badly for the attackers. His survival can only be thought of as a miracle but in fact it was due to his quick recognition and reaction to the situation and his guidance to the helicopter operator to land in the only location on the ranch that would give all of them a chance to survive.

The location was the very pond where he had taken his wife for their first skinny dip. I love the story of the Admiral's love affair and often go over it and would gladly digress but that is a story that is not pertinent in this account.

I would be remiss if I did not give a great deal credit to the skill of the helicopter pilot and copilot. Their combined skills were required in bringing down a very damaged craft in a manner that allowed them all to survive. They skimmed the helicopter across the pond and into the far bank where it flipped upside down. It was a water landing that kept the flames from engulfing the hilo.

It is an account that also highlights the resilience and the response attack that the Admiral brought to everything he did. It highlights his ability to immediately lead his followers into the mouth of danger and their willingness to follow him. As I read the account I personally envisioned myself following him. He definitely was the kind of person that I personally have dreamt of working for.

But let me not digress, I am focused on a moment that was a traumatic event that seems to have hardly interrupted the work that the Admiral had returned to Earth to get done. He was able to return with the information that revolutionized the Cosmos fleet. The attack serves to provide the historic tapestry that reveals to the core the type of individual the Admiral was. He was inspirational, he was dynamic, he was THE Admiral. He was destined to be the person who revealed that the Human fabric spanned multiple galaxies and nine planets that resided in those galaxies.

****

Nojus sat his South San Antonio apartment at his desk pouring over the global news and keeping track of the movement of the seven Cosmos ships.

He had one screen to track each of the seven ships though the new configuration that had four ships combined into one had him showing the same image on four screens. He had hacked into the Lakland Airbase tracking system and always had the latest information about the ships. He was especially interested in the fact that the sphere that consisted of four ships had just reappeared. It was clear to him as he monitored the communication between the Quartet, as the four were referred to and ground control that it was a surprise return.

This triggered his plan to earn the fifty million dollar bounty that had been put on Five Star Admiral Joseph Elsinger's head. He had no clue where the money came from but he had been able to secure ten percent when he had shared his plan with the contact that had approached him. When he asked why they had approached him he learned that one of his obscure posts about the fact that he could break through any firewall currently being used had attracted the attention of his unknown benefactor.

He had followed the trail his contact had left to ensure himself that it was not a trap and then accepted the offer.

They put five million dollars into his off shore Vanuatu bank account and had assured him the rest of the money would be sent to the bank once he completed the contract.

He thought about his grandfather who had been arrested in Lithuania during the Second World War for his attempt to assassinate Soviet Army Commander Zhukova. He smiled and thought of himself as a chip off of his grandfather's old block.

He unlike his grandfather was not doing it for god and country but he was doing it for the sake of making millions and then heading for one of Vanuatu's eighty islands in the Pacific where he would spend the rest of his day's enjoying the sun, surf, sipping on cold beer and hopefully enjoying the company of some attractive women.

He had established a small team, purchased two surface to air missiles, a flatbed truck to transport and launch the missiles that he planned to utilize to shoot down the hilo that always transported the Admiral to and from the ranch where he had grown up.

He had practiced positioning the truck along the small highway that went by the ranch. He knew that the truck would be a sitting duck once it fired its missiles so he had a small motorcycle carrier that would allow he and his team to abandon the truck once they fired the missiles. He felt very confident that the confusion that would follow blowing the hilo out of the sky over the ranch would provide the means to get to the airfield where his private plan was kept.

When he saw the sphere appear he activated his team and they drove the truck out to the ranch to wait for the hilo to appear.

Joe and Lydia were chatting with Tyler and Veetry as they made the normal approach to the ranch.

Jow glanced out and saw a large flatbed truck with what appeared to be two missiles mounted on it. He immediately gave the order to dive to the surface.

Tyler heard the order and took the chopper into a steep dive.

Veetry looked around and shouted out, "missile."

The hilo swerved and got spun around as the missile streaked by, brushed the hilo and then exploded.

Joe shouted to the dive for the pond.

Tyler had the hilo at top speed as he skimmed along the ground. It had almost reached the pond when the explosion of the second missile seemed to launch the hilo in an uncontrolled way toward the ground. He used what little control was left to tilt the hilo forward toward the surface of the pond. He watched as the water surged around the front of the hilo and then hit a rock at the edge of the pond and caused it to flip and turn over on its top. He heard the rotating blades shattering and then everything was still.

Joe watched as Tyler brought the hilo in a controlled crash into the pond. As soon as the hilo stopped at the edge of the pond he unbuckled his safety harness and stood on the roof of the upside down hilo and helped Lydia get down and out. He then helped both Veetry and Tyler get out as well. He verified that no one had any injuries. Then he climbed up and looked out to where the truck was located.

A herd of cattle was peacefully eating grass between the four of them and the truck. He shouted for the three to follow him. He pointed his left and told Veetry to run on the left side of the herd, he pointed to his right and told Lydia to run the right and then pointed at Tyler and told him to run behind the herd but to his left. The four of them ran rapidly across the field and got the herd moving toward the truck.

The herd of cattle took off and were soon running at full speed. Joe saw that his father had made the fence along the highway a wooden one painted white. He was now shouting as loud as could urging the cattle to run faster. He saw that the men on the truck were firing at them. He saw Veetry get hit stumble but keep running. A moment later Tyler jerked sidewards but kept running. Joe was not surprised when he too was hit. He gritted his teeth and chose to run faster. The herd hit the fence and it exploded and threw pieces of the timber at him like spears trying to skewer him. The middle of the herd hit the side of the truck and cause the men standing on the flat bed to fall.

Joe jumped up on the truck with a piece of the fence that he used to skewer one of the shooters. He broke the piece in half and hit a second shooter on the side of his head. He watched a third shooter fall backwards off the flat bed. The fourth person jumped on a motor cycle and headed down the highway.

As he was off loading a cycle to chase down the figure riding away he saw that Lydia had gone under the truck and had pushed the shooter that had fallen down out into the flow of the cattle where he was getting thoroughly stomped. He doubted the shooter would survive. Lydia picked up the shooter's rifle, threw it to him, and then sat down by one of the rear wheels of the truck.

Lydia had run along on her side of the herd, shouting at the top of her voice to keep the cattle running. She saw Veetry, then Tyler and Joe get hit and had raised her voice as she expected to be the next one to be hit.

As she approached the truck the herd passed more toward the back. She dove under the truck and saw one of the shooters fall down. She jump up from under the truck, picked up the rifle the shooter had dropped and hit him with the butt and then pushed him out into the passing herd. She watched as Joe dropped off the flatbed as he readied to ride a black motorcycle after the fourth person that was speeding away down the highway. She tossed him the rifle she had in her hand, watched him catch it in a bloody hand as she sat down.

Veetry staggered the last few steps around the front of the truck and dropped down by the front wheel. She knew that she was going to pass out. She looked to her left and saw Lydia sitting by the rear wheel and then passed out.

Tyler came around behind Veetry and dropped down beside her and put a pressure on her leg wound that was bleeding. He was having trouble breathing but was more worried about her than himself. He felt that they were going to make it if they could survive long enough to get their wounds looked at.

Lydia walked over and was about to see what she could do when she heard Uncle Ted ask who was in need of help. She pointed to Veetry and Tyler and sat down on the road. She knew that all of them had just lived through a miracle. She was now worried about Joe.

Trey had observed Joe riding away on a motorcycle and figured he should drive the pickup after him. He handed Lydia a bottle of water and said he would be back. He then jumped behind the wheel and took the pickup to its top speed. He looked over at Pedro who was clutching the handle at the top of the door.

Joe knew he had been hit but he was not bleeding much. He ripped off a piece of his shirt that had ripped during the crash and jammed it into the wound in his side as he rode at top speed after the motor bike that he could see in front of him.

Nojus was doing the best he could to make his getaway. He had been surprised that the hilo had been able to survive the two missiles. What surprised him even more was when he realized that an entire herd of cattle was stampeding toward the truck and all four persons on the hilo were pushing the herd. He was more upset that his three shooters had so much trouble picking off four unarmed people. He got his cycle ready for his getaway as the cattle hit the fence. He figured he would make his escape and left his three team members to handle the situation on their own. He looked back and was amazed to see someone following him. He wondered if it was one of his crew. As the cycle behind him got closer, he heard what he thought might be a shot being fired. He decided it was not one of his crew and bent forward on his bike trying to get more speed.

Esoteric Journey

Joe was leaning forward as low as he could over the handle bars of the bike. He had the throttle full open and could see that he was closing the distance to the bike ahead of him. He could not aim but he fired the rifle toward the fleeing cycle. He saw where the bullet skipped on the pavement. He readjusted the rifle and fired again. This time the person on the cycle got hit and lost control of the cycle. The cycle and the person went tumbling and bouncing down along the highway. It seemed to be a contest of between the two to see which would out bounce and out roll the other. Joe brought his cycle to a stop when he reached the now broken and still body. He had just dismounted his cycle when the pickup driven by his father and a ranch hand drove up. It was then that he sat sideways on the bike seat and realized that he was out of Schlitz and about ready to pass out. He wondered just how much blood he had lost.

Trey knew he was driving like a mad man as he drove down the highway. He looked over at Pedro who was still holding on to the handled above the door with one hand and had put his other hand on the dashboard. Pedro was one of the younger cousins of Fabio who was now a Chef on one of the Cosmos ships. Pedro had only been on the ranch a couple of years. Trey saw Joe stop and saw the figure sprawled out on the highway and knew that whoever it was, was dead. He got out and asked Joe if he was alright. He took pictures of the scene and asked Pedro to move the mangled cycle to the side of road. He then positioned the pickup so the two of them could put the body into the bed of the pickup. He got Joe to sit in the passenger seat and he asked Pedro to ride the operating cycle back to the ranch.

He drove back to where the flatbed truck was. The rest of the crew was gathered around the three figures on the ground. He got two of them to take the body out of the pickup and put it up on the flat bed. He saw the body behind the flatbed, took pictures and then had that body put up on the flat bed. One of his crew let him know that one of the persons on the flat bed was still alive. He saw the flashing lights approaching and figured that the local sheriff and rescue EMT unit would soon be on hand. He decided they could deal with the live person on the flatbed.

The sheriff arrived and asked what had happened.

The EMT unit stopped and they jumped out and began checking on the wounds that each had.

Lydia stood up and said that she would explain what had happened. One of the EMT's came over to her and wiped the blood from her face and asked where she was wounded. Lydia shook her head and said she did not think the blood was hers. She looked out in the field and pointed to one of the cattle that was down, smiled and said that it had taken the bullet meant for her and it was probably its blood.

Uncle Ted looked out and told one of the ranch hands to get the steer to the barn and skin it. He was going to prepare it as the main course for the evening meal. He then let each of the EMT's know that his three patients were going to be just fine but he had not bothered to look at the single surviving attacker that was up on the bed of the truck.

One of the EMT's opened up Joe's shirt and let him know that he was lucky that the bullet had traveled through and though there had been a lot of bleeding it did not seem to have hit a major blood vessel or organ.

Joe thanked him and then asked Tyler to call for another chopper to take them all back to Lakland so they could go through the Door. After doing that they would all return and enjoy one of Uncle Ted's steak dinners.

Tyler made the call but he added instructions to have one of the Sikorski Hilos come and take what was left of his hilo out of the pond. He also suggested that a recovery team be assigned to pick up any scraps that might have been dropped on the ranch as the missiles exploded and parts of his hilo fell to the ground.

Joe called Jorge, gave him the details of the attack, and asked him to arrange with Doug to hold a prisoner that they would want to interrogate to find out what they could about the attack.

Jorge talked with Doug and they agreed that they would fly out and get a firsthand look at the attack site and see what they could learn from what was there.

It was not long before the ranch seemed to be overrun with personnel in Intergalactic Space Force uniforms. Before the sun set, the pond was cleared, the fields were being scoured, the scrap metal was being retrieved, the cattle were herded back to their field and a temporary fence put up. It would likely take another couple of days to get everything totally cleaned up but the majority got done that day.

Uncle Ted made sure all the personnel were invited for a grilled steak, a potato and as much iced tea as they wanted to drink.

Jorge and Doug stayed for steak as well.

Joe, Lydia, Tyler and Veetry returned to Lakland and traveled through the Door. As always, the transit repaired all wounds. They returned weary but ready to enjoy their steak dinner.

Uncle Ted had all the service personnel out on the lawn and had dinner for Joe and the rest up on the Veranda.

Joe took a minute to thank everyone for their quick response and help in getting the ranch back into shape. He then took time to elaborate how the two best hilo pilots in the force had saved he and Lydia's life.

Jorge listened and once again knew why Joe was a Five Star Admiral. He had been the one that had led his team to defeat the attackers but he instead praised the people that had followed his lead. He recalled having come to the ranch to recruit Joe and was pleased that he had been successful.

10

The Source

I continue here with a deeper analysis of the follow up based on the failed attack on the Admiral's life. The Admiral got everyone out of the upside down helicopter and then led them in what I can only describe as a maniacal, unarmed attack on the men responsible for shooting down the helicopter. The Admiral, and the two helicopter pilots were all wounded by the attackers whose missiles had missed killing them but who directly shot at them as they all ran a herd of cattle towards the truck that had been the launch pad for the missiles that had brought the helicopter down.

Lydia, the Admiral's wife was the only one that was not wounded but who ended up with the most blood on her. It is one of the few amusing things about the assassination attempt. She was able to point to one of the cattle that had been killed and make the statement that she had a faithful defender that had taken a bullet for her. The record shows that the steer she pointed out and several others ended up being grilled by Uncle Ted and served to all the Cosmos personnel that ended up at the ranch to clean out the debris from the attack.

10 The Source

Once again the Admiral was able to turn certain calamity into a positive result. He was able to utilize the healing power of the Door to rebound from the attack. He rewarded the two pilots with promotion and to a permanent assignment as the operators of his new helicopter. He used what had appeared to be a setback to accelerate the Cosmos journey of discovery.

Again, this is the type of person that I can only dream of following.

However, what seems to be missing in the record is the source of the persons funding the assassination attempt. I will need to dig deeper into other sources to see if I can determine who or what organization was behind the action.

In any case I present the best account based on the research I have so far done.

****

Emelio woke up strapped down and restrained. He could hear the chop-chop of the blades of a hilo but had trouble remembering what had happened. As the flight went on he recalled firing the missile to down the hilo and watching as the hilo took a dive and evaded the missile. He remembered that Sam had a little better luck and was able to knock the hilo out of the air. He had watched the hilo disappear and then a few moments later a fire ball had risen from the ground. Then he recalled seeing a herd of cattle racing toward the flat bed where he was standing. He didn't think much of it and took up shooting at the four people that were driving the herd toward the truck.

He was sure he hit the female running on the left side of the herd and was surprised that she had only missed a step and then was running full speed again. He figured he would get back to her after shooting the other woman. He took a shot at the woman on the other side and must have missed when he saw one of the cows stumble and fall.

What took him by surprise was when the herd smashed through the fence, hit, and almost overturned the flat bed.

What he witnessed next was a mad man with a piece of the fence drive it through Herb's chest and then hit him on the side of the head. The next thing he recalled was being strapped to the board he was on. He now had no idea where he was. He wondered what had happened to his boss Nojus and whether he would get the thousand dollars bonus he had been promised.

Less and Jack were waiting for the hilo coming from the ranch with the only living member of the attack team. They had received orders from their boss to take the person being brought to the base and get him transported through the Door. They knew from their own experience that the transport would heal any wounds. Once they had the person transported back from the Door, they were to put him in a holding cell until he could be interrogated. Doug had also freed them to use their imagination on how to intimidate the prisoner. They learned that he was the single live person who had attacked the Admiral, Lydia and two hilo pilots. They discussed just how "gently" they should handle their prisoner.

Joe, Lydia, Tyler and Veetry arrived at the Door building a few moments before Less and Jack brought their prisoner there. They each traveled through the Door and then returned. They were just getting ready to leave when Less and Jack arrived with their prisoner. It was clear that the two of them were not being gentle with the person that they were holding between them.

Joe walked over to them, said hello to the two of them and then asked the person with them what his name was.

From pictures Nojus had shown him, Emilio knew he was talking to the Admiral that they were supposed to assassinate. He replied that he was Emilio. He wondered what kind of threat he was going to face.

The Admiral nodded and said that he would be back to talk with him and when he did Emilio should understand that if he did not cooperate he had the authority to sentence him to death. He should think about that until the day the two of them met again. Emilio then heard the Admiral tell the two that were holding him that they knew how to appropriately treat their prisoner.

Joe walked back to where Lydia and his two pilots were standing and asked if they were ready to fly to the ranch once again. When they got to the hilo flight building he walked over to the person in charge and asked whether the new hilo that he had ordered had been processed and might be ready for use. He was assured that the new hilo had been processed and was ready for use but there were no pilots available. Joe pointed to Veetry and Tyler and replied that he had two newly promoted pilots with him that would be the exclusive pilots of the new helicopter.

Veetry walked over to the hilo and opened all the doors as she walked around following the red, blue, and white strip on the body of the otherwise sparkling black helicopter. She commented that the four extra wide seats with armrests that had a console between the seats were especially nice. The front two passenger seats were turned to face the two in the rear that faced forward. She patted the pilot and copilot seats that were of the same comfortable design and smiled broadly.

She got in and looked over the controls and shared that it could fly at one hundred seventy miles per hour and had a five hundred mile range. She added that with an auxiliary tank it had another three hundred mile range.

Tyler inspected the turboshaft engines, the main gearbox with run-dry capability; noted the hilo featured four-blade, rigid, composite main rotor blades, an upgraded style composite main rotor hub that was a four-blade design. He pointed out the composite tail rotor; graphite tail boom; and tail rotor drive shaft and said that it was of the latest design. He patted the hilo on the nose and said that it was the most beautiful hilo he had ever seen. He added that it was certainly better than he had ever piloted.

Joe nodded and said he was glad that the two of them liked their new hilo that he was permanently assigning them to and a hilo they would not have to fight to pilot since they would be the two primary pilots both who were as of the moment promoted to the rank of Lieutenant Commanders to be his personal, permanent hilo pilots.

Lydia congratulated them on their promotion, shook their hands and asked if they were ready to fly back to the ranch.

Back on the ranch, Uncle Ted got an estimate on the number of persons working to clean the debris from the ranch. He had the ranch hands bring in one more head in and butcher it so they would have enough to feed what had been estimated to be around one hundred personnel.

He had the ranch hands all working with him to prepare a reward dinner for everyone that had come out to the ranch to gather the wreckage that was left after the attack. He planned for them to gather out on the lawn and sit wherever they desired.

Trey had gone out to the pond to watch the cleanup there. He was amazed that anyone had managed to survive and then be able to orchestrate a retaliatory response. He was looking forward to listening to how that had happened. He knew ahead of time that he would have to rely on Lydia and the two pilots to tell him the story because Joe would simplify his response and simply say that they had done the only logical thing to do. He did not accept that running a herd of cattle toward men shooting at you as a logical thing to do.

He asked those that were lifting the hilo out of the pond to make sure to get all parts out of the bottom and then as he rode back to the house he heard the very different sound of another helicopter. He looked up to see a sparkling black hilo landing on the ranches hilo pad. He rode over and got off his horse and handed the reins to Jose who had run out to take her back into the barn.

He watched as Lydia jumped out followed by Joe. The hilo was turned off and the two pilots emerged and joined Lydia and Joe.

Trey walked around the hilo and when he got back to the four he jokingly suggested that crashing a very good hilo into the pond was a crazy way to upgrade to a new sleek super charged one.

Joe gave his dad a hug and said that was the only thing he had come up with to justify the upgrade and he hoped that it did not cause his father to be disappointed. He then formally introduced Lieutenant Commanders Veetry Rao and Tyler Randle.

Trey laughed and said that he might have to change his mind about the motive for crashing a perfectly good hilo into the pond. He went on to say that it might have been to get promoted as he congratulated the two.

Lydia shook her head and said that he had it all wrong, the four of them had conspired to have Uncle Ted have the type of large gathering that he loved to feed and having one of the steers to take a bullet for her was really the whole intent of stampeding the cattle.

Trey shook his head and replied that she had succeeded in making Ted very happy and then led the way toward the house.

10 The Source

Jorge and Doug came back after having walked most of the afternoon getting a firsthand look at the scene of the hilo crash, the location of the missile laden truck, the post-mortem field examinations of the three bodies and the initial missile part findings. They commented that they were going to share a steak with four of the luckiest people they knew.

The smell of the grilling steaks energized their pace as they approached the house.

Doug looked at Jorge and commented that he hoped he would be able to have seconds.

Jorge laughed and said that asking for seconds was the high praise that always caused Uncle Ted to offer more of everything. When they reached the Veranda Jorge pointed to two seats that were empty and as he walked toward them asked if they were taken.

Uncle Ted was in the process of putting a steak down in front of Veetry and said that he would have their plates out to them in a sec. He asked if they were hungry enough for a three ounce steak and smiled as he walked back into the kitchen. When he returned he apologized that he had no three ounce steaks and they would each have to accept a twenty ounce one.

Jorge looked out toward the barn and saw the grill there smoking and a long table with cuts of beef, baked potatoes, and a variety of other grilled vegetables. He gave up counting all the service men and women sitting around on the lawn enjoying a great meal.

He knew that Uncle Ted was going to feel great about having fed all the people that were working on the ranch. He would need to make sure that the meals were expensed and billed to the Cosmos account.

After a few bites and a sip of his wine, Doug commented that he had received a call from Less and Jack who had asked how rough they should handle their current prisoner. He looked around and then said that he had instructed them to threaten but keep their hands off because they needed the prisoner to give them a clue to who might have funded the attempted assassination. He added that if they didn't get the information that they needed from the prisoner they might tag him and release him to see if the people behind the effort tried to either take him off line or tried to kill him. He smiled and said that both Less and Jack said they could go back to one of the Cosmos ships and monitor him from there and track whoever might take him.

Joe waited for a moment and when Uncle Ted was back on the veranda said the he was open to Less's and Jack's ideas and then added that if the two were to go out to one of the Cosmos ships he was sorry that they would have to suffer the gruel served by the Chef's trained by Uncle Ted.

Uncle Ted shook his head, feigned wiping away tears and said that was what he got for raising Joe in such a poor manner. He then looked around the table and asked how the gruel was that he was serving and they were all eating.

10 The Source

11

Tirayidi of Bintang

The next chapter of the Admiral's travel takes him to the fifth human seeded world. It is also a point in time that he acts to change the condition of the world that his team discovered. He had developed his team in such a fashion that they were constantly gaining new skills. One of those skills was the ability to hack into the computer systems of the space craft that they faced. This was not a skill that the Admiral had worked at developing but a skill that was embedded in several of the people that were in his crew. It was a skill that had greatly benefited the Cosmos team in the visit to the fourth human planet and once again did so in the visit to the fifth one.

The records show that the Cosmos hackers had been able to lift the ability to generate gravity from the beings on the fourth seeded planet. When they faced the beings seeded on the fifth planet they were able to again hack into the computer systems and discover the plans for a more efficient gravity generator system but also an enhanced propulsion and a much cheaper shielding system.

The information that they uncovered was one that they took immediately back to Earth so it could be incorporated into the next generation of Cosmos ships.

11 Tirayidi of Bintang

I was impressed with the hacking capability that rose to the surface and became so important to the continuing journey of discovery. The information about the human cousins that they were meeting became increasingly important as they faced technology that seemed each time to be more challenging.

But let me refocus on the Admiral. It was during the interaction with the leaders that were in power on the fifth planet that the Admiral's bias against oppressive regimes surface in a manner that had him taking small but direct action to change the situation. He would not lead a revolt against the totalitarian regime but in fact would subtly position a person who would in fact end up being the George Washington of that planet.

As I continually express my admiration for the Admiral I realize that I am becoming more and more biased in my assessments.

****

His scientific officer had notified him of the lasers that had mysteriously appeared were apparently cleansing a large area of space of dust and other small particles. Riccart was now arguing with the Tirayidi about the fact that he had ordered the personnel on the Dili to monitor but take no action. The Tirayidi were arguing among themselves and with him about his wait and see attitude. The hotter members wanted to immediately destroy the lasers. A few were on the side of wait and see. He had the Dili moving out towards the area being cleared. His actions were in fact rather rapid in that less than three seconds had passed before he let the Tirayidi know that he was positioning the Dili within a few seconds of striking range.

He felt confident that the armament that the Dili carried was sufficient to defeat any threat it might be presented with.

Joe had returned to the Cosmos Quartet that now had the gravity generators. He had it fly several random patterns as he walked around the wheel that was no longer rotating. He was impressed with the fact that Jerry and his engineering team had been able to so rapidly produce and have the gravity generators installed . He knew that Jerry was in the process of purchasing a huge rocket from one of the private firms that was having problems with producing a large enough engine to launch it into space. The rocket once modified internally would be large enough that all four of the crews on the Quartet would have ample room. Jerry's team had also taken the idea of having gravity generators positioned so that gravity would always have a person standing in such a manner that there feet would be toward the outer hull of the rocket. The interior of the rocket would have four floors and would have three hundred sixty degree gravity. He wondered how that would affect a person when they were to walk around and enjoy the feel of gravity on every level.

He brought his mind back to the walk he was taking on the Voyager. He was looking forward to having a new ship but for now he had to focus on the upcoming journey to find the fifth seeded planet.

Lydia, Samantha, Yara and Lacey were discussing the change and what the gravity generators provided the Quartet.

Yara commented that repurposing the engines that had provided the rotational power to provide additional thrust for the Quartet was estimated to give it forty percent greater speed.

Samantha suggested they take the Quartet for a test run at that greater speed to see how that would feel.

Lacey agreed and suggested that they do it immediately before they went through the next Hole.

Joe heard the call to stations for trajectory practice and returned to the control room. He took his seat as the Quartet went into the random flight pattern at full speed. He noticed that the turns required to maintain the pattern required extra course adjustments due to the increased speed. What caught his attention was that the gravity generator control systems all adjusted to maintain a one G force even when the ship was taking a sharp turn that would have caused the force to have increased. The people in the interior of the ship did not feel any of the G forces. He felt like giving a shout out to the inventors of the gravity generators and certainly to Jerry's engineering team for having been able to produce and so rapidly install them.

When the lasers stopped firing, turned, and pointed toward the Dili, Ricart called battle stations and had his missile operators ready to respond if any of the lasers fired. He was not sure what was about to happen but felt confident that the outer armor layer would absorb any initial assault. He had personally tested the armor layer that was designed to absorb energy and was confident that he knew of no weapon that would penetrate it.

He kept arguing with the Tirayidi when they decided that they wanted him to begin to fire at the lasers. The argument suddenly ended when a speeding sphere burst into view and went on a random flight through space. He set the Deli in chase to get a closer view. He was impressed when his navigator let him know that the sphere was not making a random flight but was following a controlled path.

He was rudely interrupted by the leader of the Tirayidi and was ordered to fire on the sphere.

He had his missile man aim for it and fire.

Lydia sat at her council watching the cleaning lasers do their job. The lasers were flashing red giving the warning that there was a large object in range. The single laser closest to that object turned and indicated the location. She gave orders to go through at max speed and away from the location of the object. She had everyone at battle stations and was ready to go into their Ropa-a-Dope flight. She took the Cosmos Quartet through and into their preprogramed flight.

Tom, H^3 and Elisha, the top computer hack were each attempting to get access to the computers of the ship that was in pursuit. They all ran into a very sophisticated fire wall. Elisha dropped back to an environmental control computer and was able to put in a line of code that she was able to augment and add one of her hacking modules. She slowly was gaining access to the ships flight control and communications systems.

Kashanti immediately sent out the visual message of friendship.

Joe monitored the progress of the rapidly approaching ship and knew that they were facing a ship that had superior fire power.

Suddenly the entire structure of the Quartet shuddered.

Lydia gave the order for the small Hole cannon to take out the engine thrusters of the ship that was chasing them.

The Hole operator fired on command and the Quartet pulled away from the ship chasing them.

Lydia brought the Quartet to a halt but remained facing the craft that had chased them.

Joe had Kashanti send a picture of the chasing ship missing its front as a warning as to what their next shot would be if attacked.

As Ricard watched the missile hit the sphere he realized that it had done minimal damage. Suddenly he saw a flash and the Dili lost all propulsion. It was floating forward on the path that it had been traveling but it no longer had any power. He recognized the explosion immediately in front of the Dili as a warning from the sphere.

The representative of the Tirayidi was screaming for him to fire more missiles. He literally had to push him away and point to the screen where his communication tech had posted a picture of the Dili with the front half missing. It had an arrow to the rear of the Dili where the entire engine area was missing. The fact that there was a weapon with the power to get through the protective gel layer and eliminate the engine area drove the meaning of the picture of the Dili missing the front section into his mind and he understood it very well.

The second picture with a person who could have been his brother holding up an empty hand was a moment that he would never forget. He had tried to destroy beings that were duplicates of himself.

They had surgically stopped him in a fashion that had spared his crew. He realized that he was facing people like himself that were indicating that they had come with friendship in mind.

He turned and had the communications tech send a picture of himself holding up his empty hand. He smiled as he realized he was using a symbol that had been used in ancient times to indicate that one did not have a weapon in hand. He envisioned the time his history teacher had brought in an iron ax used in hand to hand combat. It had made him wonder if he would have been able to march into battle swinging such a weapon. He could not imagine being able to look into a person's eyes and swing such a weapon and try to kill.

Elisha had been able to hack into the main computer and send her routine to the planet where there seemed to be a gigantic computer system that connect to various other networks. She set up a data gathering routing that grabbed lines of code and pushed into information cubes that she had set up. Her approach was to grab and go and worry about deciphering the information later. This allowed her to keep moving rapidly through lines of code before facing an defensive efforts.

Joe was relieved to get the reply with a raised empty hand. He had Kshanti initiate the communication protocol that they were now well versed in using. He added a picture of having the eight small fighter vessels acting as tug boats pushing the large ship back towards planet five.

Ricard understood the offer and sent back a picture of him putting one of the small space ships into place. He wondered how long it would take the eight small ships to push the Dili back to Kelima. He then turned and went to deal with the Tirayidi. He first sent a message to his boss and have her deal with the larger body that the Tirayidi represented. He had little patience left to deal with the five representatives that were on board. He wondered what type of leadership existed on the sphere that was now following the Dili.

Joe was in the process of examining the damage that the Cosmos Quartet shield had sustained. It was clear to him that the missile that had hit was more powerful that anything that was in his conventional arsenal and it was not a nuclear weapon. He hoped that Tom, Linda and H^3 could find the plans when they scanned the information that Elisha was dumping into the memory cubes she was currently filling. She had let him know that she would have almost all the information that was stored in the planets computer systems by the time they got into orbit around the planet.

Ricard learned of the plan to hit the sphere with a powerful rocket that would be launched from Kelima when they got closer. He advised against it but was overridden. He wondered how the beings on the sphere would react.

Samantha's navigator was the one that spotted the missile rising from the planet. She gave the order to use a laser to shoot it down.

Ricard watched as the missile rose up from the planet and about the time it cleared the exosphere a laser from the sphere hit it and the missile blew up. He shook his head as he realized that whatever contamination it would create would rain down on Kelima. He also realized that the beings on the sphere were well versed in dealing with other beings of their kind. He wondered where they came from. Their appearance had a somewhat mystical aura about them. Their power seemed to be equal to what he was aware that the people on Kelima had but they seemed to be able to concentrate their actions in such a way that they seemed much more powerful.

He looked out to where Bintang was shining and envisioned the four inner planets the closest that was a source of many minerals that fed the industrial complex on Kelima and had been the source of most of the materials that gone into the building of the Dili. He knew that the sixth planet was currently being explored for additional materials but that some life forms had been found there that had excited the group that was wondering if there was intelligent life on other planets in the star systems. He wondered what those groups would make of intelligent beings arriving in a sphere capable of incapacitating the Dili. This was more intelligence than they might have been anticipating or looking for. It certainly was more than he had ever anticipated. He had always thought of himself doing the discovery of intelligence in some far away galaxy.

Tom and Linda were pouring over the files that Elisha had put on the cubes.

H^3 let out a yell when he found what he thought was the plans for the weapon that had almost broken through their shield.

Linda was the one that verified that indeed it was the picture of the missile.

H^3 next said he had what he thought were the drawings of another gravity generator design and it appeared to be more versatile than the one they currently had the plans for.

Tom laughed and said that he had found the plans for the Door but instead of using it for transport the beings on the planet used it to generate and prepared different meals. He liked the way they had modified the equations to do so and he pointed out the point at which they had entirely missed the concept of transporting people.

During the post encounter analysis where they all discussed the effectiveness of their existing weapons and defensive systems, Linda suggested they return to Earth to share the upgrade to the gravitation generators and to have the protective coating that was on the missile like spaceship analyzed as a cheaper means of shielding the ship that Jerry was having built.

Joe agreed that they would do so as soon as they got the translation and negotiating teams established. He said that as soon as they had two Door modules orbiting the planet they would make the return trip. He suggested that Tom, Linda and H^3 return with the wealth of information that they had and let the team on Earth pour over the information. He added that doing so might expedite the new ship getting built and ready for use.

12

Revolt

What stands out about the Admiral's personal interaction with the beings on the fifth seeded planet was that he facilitated the overthrow of the authoritarian political system. He did not take any direct action, but he provided just enough support and the seed equipment that allowed for an overthrow to take place. Understandingly he kept this support very low key since he had to initially deal with the power structure currently in control of the planet.

I especially like the impact he had on the person that turned out to be the planets equivalent to himself and the love affair he saved by letting the person who he was aiding know that if wounded he should go for an immediate cure to the module that was being placed in orbit around the planet. It turned out that the person he shared that information with took the woman who he had fallen in love with and who had been shot while protecting him, to the Door module. She was transported through the Door and became the lifetime companion to the person who became that planet's next global leader.

He was a leader of the Admiral's stature and guided that world into a democratically controlled world. His love affair was one that was equivalent to the Admiral's love affair with his wife Lydia.

But let's focus on what occurred during the Admiral's visit and the information his team was able to extract through their hacking capability. It was to later play a big role in the interactions with the humans on the sixth, seventh, eighth and especially on the visit to the ninth planet. The nineth planet, my planet and one that had lost its memory of the events that led to seeding the universe with humans.

The records will show that the Admiral and his team utilized all their above board and below board talents to position themselves to always have the upper hand when dealing with skeptical or dubious individuals that they would meet in the journey to each of the nine human populations spread across the universe.

****

Jorge was alerted to the arrival of Tom, Linda and H^3, he let Jerry know and the two of them went together to the Door building where they greeted the three. It was ten in the morning so they all returned to Jorge's office. Once there, he asked the reason for their return.

Linda placed three information cubes on the table and said that they had returned with the information about the fifth planet that they felt was critical to get reviewed.

Tom added that a more efficient gravity generator was one critical technical item and what might be a rather inexpensive polymer like shielding skin for a rocket might be a second critical item.

H^3 then commented that there most likely was a ton of additional technical break throughs that would have commercial value such as a dinner meal generator. He figured the analysis team would have their hands full getting all the details examined.

Jerry asked how in such a short time the team had been able to get their hands on all the information.

H^3 chuckled and said that they had discovered a person, Elisha Sands that was one of the best computer hacks that he had ever run into. She had been able to break through the firewall and gain access to almost every computer network on the fifth planet.

Linda added that the ability to hack into the planets network system allowed them to estimate the time that the planet had been seeded. It was very clear to everyone that they were traveling in the reverse order that the planets had been seeded and that Earth had been the last in the seeding process. This meant that on each trip they potentially faced a more technologically advanced population.

She added that it would be interesting to learn if there were subtle differences in the human body that were not visible to just the looks.

Jorge nodded and added that the physical differences might not exist if the humans doing the seeding, seeded each planet with the same physical attributes.

Linda smiled and asked if the Cosmos Jet was available for her and Tom to use so they could fly to London to visit their daughter who was expecting her third child.

Jorge smiled and asked if it was a boy or girl and said that he would arrange for the flight. He looked at H^3 and asked if he had any plans.

H^3 nodded and said that he was interested in working with Jerry's technical folks in digging into the technology that was in the cubes. He was sure that the gravity generators would be a significant improvement over the technology they were getting ready to use. They appeared significantly smaller and seemed to indicate that they generated a denser gravity field.

A few star systems away, Joe was monitoring the language and political alignment process. It had become crystal clear to him that they were dealing with a global totalitarian political establishment. He kept wondering what he or the rest of his team might be able to do to change the situation.

Lacey suggested providing the opposition with information on the weaponry that the totalitarian government had kept secret and to provide funding by intercepting the shipments of valuable minerals from the fourth planet of the system.

Joe was not sure how they would enable the redirection of the shipments then during a conversation with the current commander of the ship that Samantha had disabled, he realized that the commander's sympathies were with the opposition. He set up several private meetings with the commander who he learned was call Riccart. The two of them hit it off and he was able to convey the idea of Riccart leading a rebellion.

Riccart at first did not understand who was trying to set up private communications with him. He personally had only two persons who he could trust and setting up such communications put them all at risk. However, his intuition led him to set up the meeting and once he understood what was being offered he immediately began to plan the move that he had only dreamt of. The offer was that he would be provided one of the small space going vessels that had pushed the Dili through space. It showed the small vessel approaching one of the space freight vessels leaving the fourth planet and landing on it. He knew immediately what he would do. The conversation also provided him with the fact that all the plans for the weapons on his ship were on some communication cubes that would also be provided.

Riccart worked with his two faithful partners to prepare for their departure from the Dili. They were able to determine the schedule of the next freight spaceship leaving planet four and arrange for an alternate landing site on Kelima that was controlled by the opposition. Once they had that spaceship on the ground he would continue hijacking as many of the freight spaceships as possible and have them remodeled into fighting spaceships. He was well aware of the fact that there was one battleship under construction and the damaged one missing its engines in orbit. He hoped that by the time the opposition leaders figured out what he was doing he would have four converted freight ships that would be able to stand up to at least one of the battleships. His other thought was that perhaps he could lead an attack to capture the battleship that was being built and take it over as well.

A new world of opportunity had taken root and he was going to do the most he could with the help he was getting from his new friend that had so easily defeated him.

The four Cosmos Quartet captains had supported Joe's desire to change the political power on the planet that they had learned was called Kelima. They made sure that the craft that was being turned over to the Kelima rebels was loaded with the Sparrow system and instructions on how to build it. They also had loaded the small rocket system and instruction of its use and how to build it. Finally, they provided the construction plans for the craft itself and for the shields that would protect it. They agreed that what they were providing should shift the power on Kelima rapidly in favor of the opposition. They sent the designated fighter over to the ship that they now knew was called the Dili after the majority of the Dili's crew had returned to the surface. So far they had not allowed any repair to get started on the missing engine section of the ship. They all agreed that delaying the repair would help to support the opposition.

Ricard and his two followers exited the Dili through a service hatch and approached the small fighter. They were impressed with the written instructions that were in their native language. They had learned that the beings they were interacting with were from a planet known as Earth and they were now impressed with the workmanship that they encountered on the small spacecraft. There was a sense of relief as they realized how easy controlling the craft was.

As they sped across toward the fourth planet they practiced maneuvering the craft. By the time they intercepted that space freighter, they were able to make an approach that let them land undetected on the hull near one of the exterior maintenance doors.

Ricard led the way and once they had entered the ship they shed their spacesuits. They had brought their stun guns that would incapacitate the person getting shot but was generally not lethal. They hoped to find a crew that would be mostly made up of men and women sympathetic to their cause. They were aware that the freighters were mostly staffed with workers sympathetic to the opposition but were controlled by a set of personnel that worked directly for the party in control. Every person in the control room and those carrying weapons would be the ones that the three of them would need to overcome.

He had Leland go up the right interior walk way and had Delan follow him. They were to each side of the cargo hold that went up through the center of the ship. He had Delan who had crewed on a cargo ship take the lead. Delan knew where the control area was and where the armed guards stood watch. As they got closer to the front of the ship they could hear the chatter of one of the guards as he gave orders to some workers. The way he was ordering them to get the work done made it very clear that he was disparaging and denigrating them.

He put his stun gun to the guards neck and Delan took his weapon. The crew doing the work looked at the two and were about to cheer when Delan put his finger to his lip.

12 Revolt

One of the workers stepped forward and extended her hand toward the guards weapon. Once she had it in her hands, she hit the guard with the weapon with as much force as she could generate. The guard was knocked out and fell to the deck. She grabbed the ring of keys and sat down to take the chain off her ankles. She then threw the keys to another member of the group. Leland had crossed over and said that there was a group of guards gathered on the side where he had been that were just leaning along the walkway.

The worker that had taken the guards weapon said that she was known as Redan and she would take several of her trusted friends and they would take care of the guards. Her friends turned out to all be women and it was clear that they had a grudge they planned to satisfy. That left five men taking off the chains from their ankles. They each picked up one of the tools they had been using and said that they were ready to enter the control room and take it over. The oldest looking one said that they had the only weapons they needed.

The eight of them walked across where they witnessed the four women approach the guards and one after the other they took out the guards by hitting them with the tools they had carried over. Redan had used her weapon to hit each of the guards under their chins or the side of their heads and then take their weapons. She handed each of the men a weapon and told them to use them efficiently and make sure they ended up in control of the ship. She and the women were going to make sure the guards they had taken out would wake up in the brig.

Ricard led the way toward the control room. As he approached there was a guard at the exterior of the control room. He pushed one of the men as if he were brutalizing him and said he had caught the stalwart lingering in the hallway.

The confused guard started to ask him who he was when the person Ricard had pushed hit him full force on the forehead with the butt of the weapon he was carrying. Ricard then burst through the door and ordered everyone to lay down on the floor or get shot. One of the guards began to raise his weapon when Delan shot him with his stun gun. The rest of the personnel fell to the floor. The were all taken to the brig while Ricard took over control.

Once everything had settled down he asked Redan if they had all the guards locked up and if everyone else was loyal to the opposition. Once that was cleared up he asked if she or anyone knew how to communicate with the leaders of the opposition and if there was a landing site on Kelima where they could put the cargo ship down.

Redan called several of the men forward and after a brief discussion she gave him the call designation of a key opposition leader.

Before establishing the communication, he asked Leland and Delan to return to the small fighter and be ready to protect the freighter from a surface missile. He reminded them that there were two systems on the small fighter that were supposed to be capable of downing a missile.

Once they had reviewed how to use the weapons they should let him know and he would establish communication. He told them that he was sure that they would need to shoot down a missile otherwise their entire effort would have been a futile effort.

Redan shook her head and asked how he had been able to get his hands on such a craft.

Riccart shook his head and replied that he would be glad to tell her the story if she would have dinner with him once they were on the ground. That story led to one of the planets historic changes in the controlling political structure and it blossomed into a cherished and often told love story between the two.

13

Positive Change

Records show that the Admiral was aware that he was traveling up a technological ladder. It was a ladder that he had little doubt could be climbed but it was also a ladder that might hold unwelcome surprises if he was not ready. He was comfortable in placing new rungs onto the ladder that were rungs contributed by the planets he was visiting. The addition of gravitation, of improved propulsion, of additional shielding and of more powerful weapons were all absorbed in a manner that became a practiced norm. The move to a large missile shape design was not his first choice since he envisioned a spherical design as potentially the more appropriate design for space travel. However, it is recorded that the Admiral was very pleased with the new rocket shape that featured significantly more space, radial gravity, internalized missile systems and two layers of shielding.

He had insisted on an personnel exercise course that made a circuit through the entire ship. Records show that it and the crews mess area were the two most utilized features.

The other feature of the ship was that it had sixteen fighting locations that were positioned along the length of the ship. These positions were capable of being remotely controlled and able to operate autonomously if required. The maneuverability of ship was a key feature that was enhanced when the Admiral took it out on the many practices that he insisted on before he was willing to take it through the next Hole.

I was personally impressed with the fact that he insisted that the ship should be able to execute a three hundred sixty degree turn while rotating on its long axis, firing the Sparrow weaponry, and hitting the targets that they were intended to hit. That requirement led to the mounting of more than two dozen navigational jets to provide such maneuverability. He also wanted to ensure that the kitchen would have no pans of food sliding about during such maneuvers.

This was a moment in time when Rear Admiral Gerald Delaney is on record stating that he had never worked so hard to satisfy any person, even his wife, like he worked to satisfy the Admiral. He is said to have praised his technical team for doing the impossible when they delivered on all the requirements.

Finally, a fact that I almost missed because it was only a foot note in the record was that the fifth planet of the Izulite star system had a huge abundance of gold. The Admiral had the gold mined, enriched, and brought to Earth to finance the entire Cosmos program. He privately worked with the US President to slowly take all records of the US financing the program.

He had his eye to moving the Cosmos Program to the Izulite system so it could become a neutral independent program that would be managed to serve all the planets that he was discovering.

This really made me realize to what extent his vision reached out into the future. He is a person who lifted himself above personal biases and looked out to a horizon of what was good for all.

****

Joe returned to orbit around Earth ready to make the move from the Cosmos Quartet to the new USS Cosmos Javelin. He went on an inspection tour of the spaceship that the Cosmos program had purchased and modified. It was located in Texas on its own private launch pad. During the tour he insisted on having an exercise and running track installed. He was pleased with the overall design and commented that he was looking forward to getting it out into space and taking it through its paces. He made the point that he wanted to improve the capability of his continuing journey because each additional seeded planet seemed to move he and the crew a hundred thousand years farther up the technological ladder and so as they stepped up the next rung they had been challenged by the humans that they had encountered.

Yara asked which of the current Captains, aside from Lydia would he see at the helm of the Javelin.

Joe nodded and said that for the next trip he would like to have all four captains on board and have them rotate in commanding it. He was going to ensure that at least three additional Javelin class ships would get built and the current captains would then be assigned to them.

13 Positive Change

The added that current second in command of the Odyssey, Endeavor and Ambassador would be promoted and become their captains. The current Cosmos ships would operate independently and would be assigned to establishing the Nivians on their new planet.

He went on to ask each of the four current captains to identify the people they wanted to bring with them from each ship. He was sure that most of the team that had started the program together would be on the list. He personally called out Fabio, Emiliano as the two Chefs that were to be part of the crew.

He then left for the ranch where he was enjoying training a new horse . It was going to be his main ride. It was a pure black Arabian. He was also training a pure white Camarillo that would be Lydia's. They would continue to ride Yin and Yang but slowly work their two new horses in and let Yin and Yang enjoy their remaining years.

He and Lydia were both working on what the names of their new horses would be.

Lydia suggested that her new horse should be called Tui the name of a white Koi that meant the spirit of the moon. She suggested that the black be call La the name for a black Koi.

Joe chuckled and said that he just realized that he was not training two pure bred horses but two fish for them to ride. He was handling the black and he began to use his name, "La, La, La" as he had him circling the center of the pen. He smiled and said that the black seemed to like his name.

They were walking toward the house together when Joe received a call that the Javelin had been launched and was in orbit. He looked at Lydia and asked if she was ready to see what handling the Javelin would be like.

Lydia shook her head in the affirmative, smiled and asked how many days of handling he was thinking about.

Joe smiled and said that would be until the four captains said they knew how to handle every maneuver they had performed with the Cosmos Quartet and any of the tests the kitchen staff had identified as a test of stability.

A few days later, all the personnel that would make up the crew of the Javelin were in place. There were a few more weapons personnel and a few more maintenance staff but eighty percent of the personnel had been on the Cosmos Quartet. Everyone commented on the additional space. Joe was pleased with the ease with which everyone settled into their roles on the new equipment and computer control systems.

After thirty grueling days of near impossible maneuvers and battle exercises he called a meeting of the captains.

Lacey was the first to speak up about the fact that they had learned to make the Javelin fly in more than a straight line but every maneuver would have been easier and less of a challenge if the ship had been a sphere.

Joe listened as every one of the captains vocally agreed and strongly suggested a sphere versus a cylindrical shape.

Yara added that they would also use less fuel and would move through the exercises much more quickly.

Joe smiled and asked if he should change the specification for the next ship to be spherical.

That got a resounding, "Voya, Voya, Voya" from all four captains.

Jerry had informed him that he was out of funds and if there were to be more ships build they would need to get more money.

Joe had learned from his longtime supporter, Jeffery Yang currently the captain of the Cosmos Empowerer that the planet Madorite in the Izulite solar system had huge deposits of gold, silver, and platinum. Jeffery had added that when the Nivian leaders had learned of the value this was to Joe they had volunteered to share fifty percent that was mined with the Cosmos Program.

Joe asked Jeffery to step into the role of Cosmos Wealth Manager and that he should obtain enough gold and the other minerals to pay for three new Cosmos spaceships.

He called a meeting with Jorge and Jerry and let them know that funding for the Cosmos program was shifting and would be handled by Jeffery. He also attended a private meeting with President Lebak to inform him of the change in funding for the Cosmos Program and verified the President's interest in becoming the first leader of the Intergalactic Association of Worlds. The headquarters for this organization would be located in orbit around the planet Madorite in the Izulite star system. As part of that transition Joe asked the

President to slowly take the Cosmos program out of his budget and to reduce the reference to it to a minimum in all records.

Jorge and Jerry were enthusiastic supporters of the move of command to what they had learned from Joe was to be a neutral organization eventually staffed by personnel from all worlds that became members. It would most likely use the planet Madorite as the location for brick and mortar facilities but he cautioned that the journey was about halfway done and there might be a better planet for them to settle on.

Jerry had asked what had caused him to change his mind about additional spaceships of rocket design. He added that his engineering team had pressed him about a rocket shape versus the more efficient and stronger spherical shape.

Joe smiled and said that he was advised by his very talented four captains that a spherical shape would perform better and be easier to handle. He added that he knew better than to argue with four of his captains and Jerry's engineering team.

Jorge laughed and said that he was sure that was exactly how history would record the change from rocket design to a sphere. He added that there would likely be a foot note about the fact that Joe had become a swash buckling pirate that had obtained enough of a gold treasure to take over the entire Cosmos operation and move it to his own select world in another galaxy and solar system.

Joe chose to ask if Jerry and Jorge planned to make the move from Earth to a world in some distant galaxy.

Jorge nodded and said that question had come up several times at the dinner table and presented a family social challenge. He added that Jerry and he had talked about this point and how it might be handled not only in their two families but in the families of all the Cosmos employees.

Joe nodded and said he understood the challenge because he planned on making the move but he was not planning to cut the ties with his family and the land that he had grown up on. He said that for the time that the members from Earth were the majority of the staffing of the Cosmos program. He would be granting leave to those personnel to make the transition through the Door back to Earth from where ever in the Universe they might happen to be.

He then pointed out that as the Cosmos Program matured it would slowly be integrating personnel from all the worlds that had humans on them and there would likely be personnel from the beings that had a different origin. The three of them, the current captains and many of the senior Earth personnel would slowly be replaced with younger persons. Eventually there would be a balanced mix of beings from multiple worlds that would be running the Cosmos Program and all the branches that were yet to be identified and implemented.

Jorge looked over to Jerry, laughed and said that his days were numbered and not too far in the future he would be led out in the desert and let loose.

14

Meeting of the Minds

My continuing research uncovered the fact that the move to establish an Intergalactic Association of Worlds that would represent every member equally was definitely an action that was led by the Admiral. He understood well that money talked and he leveraged the wealth that the very grateful Nivians were very willing to share. He had multiple spherical spaceships built and moved into position away from Earth so that he as the leader of the Intergalactic Space Force would have time to allow the Intergalactic Association of Worlds to get established and staffed by people from the worlds that he was discovering.

The record is clear that he had listened to his captains and the Engineers that designed his spaceships and all subsequent Cosmos spaceships were spherical in their design. One subtle design twist was having a section of the sphere that resembled a saucer design capable of flying in both space and in the atmosphere of a planet. This capability became very important when the Admiral finally arrived at my planet and faced strong opposition to his friendly but firm demand that the establishers of the eight human colonies remember why they had done so.

14 Meeting of the Minds

It was a memory that I personally needed to dig deep into my planets history to find the reason we were the seeders of the other eight planets. It was a social memory that the Admiral's staff had found in the records that had been so deeply buried in my planets data bases that they were found on computers that had been mothballed in a repository and forgotten. That reason was to become the next great venture of the Cosmos Fleet.

But as is my bad habit, I have wandered ahead and into information that will be important when the Admiral finally arrives at the summit of the eight sided pyramid that is guiding him.

What is important to focus on is the meeting he had with the space commander of the sixth planet. Yes, the Admiral was taking his missile shaped spaceship and would face a spherical spaceship that once again would challenge him. It would demonstrated the maneuverability that his four captains had verbalized. The spherical spaceship, however, would not have the multiple layers of shielding enjoyed by the Cosmos Javelin nor would it have the overall fire power that the Admiral had accumulated from the previous worlds he had visited.

What became apparent to both the personnel on the Javelin and the personnel of the spherical spaceship was that the Javelin was as good at maneuvering in space as any spherical vessel. The people on the Javelin knew that the practice, practice, practice that the Admiral had put them through allowed them to demonstrate a performance that made the leaders on the spherical vessel hesitated to directly confront.

The Admiral is on record as having given his team orders to gain control of the humans they faced in the spherical vessel and to do it before there was a power face off. He reminded them that in all probability they had jumped technologically forward in time more than one hundred thousand years and they were like the English in the Battle of Agincourt where they faced a superior French army that outnumbered them three to one but had prevailed through shear use of an integrated battle plan and in the end won the battle. In fact, the English king was made the King of France as well as England.

On record the Admiral is said to have asked his team to lead the charge and gain control of not only the rather unfriendly, superior behaving humans they were communicating with on the spaceship but of the systems that controlled the communications and economic systems of the planetary home of the Sphere.

The new technology that the team discovered as they took the action ordered by the Admiral was the ability to communicate mentally that required no interpretation. This ability was a revolutionary step in how to interact with the humans they were interfacing with and essentially ended the need for long, tedious learning of the other language.

His team's ability to hack into the sixth colony's computer system was the edge that overcame the technological gap. The Admiral was then able to exert appropriate influence to establish a relationship of equals and pull them into the Intergalactic Association of Worlds.

****

14 Meeting of the Minds

Joe sat at the Javelin's control center and took in the view the camera in the Hole cannon provided. It was aimed at a point in the sky with the coordinates that had been provided by Linda, Tom and H^3.

Samantha had drawn the short straw and was the captain that would be the first to take the Javelin through to the star system where the sixth human colony was located. She had decided to go through in what appeared to be a random tumble. The cleaning lasers were sent through and when they completed their laser cleansing of the area that the Javelin would transit they all pointed to an upward direction with the indication of a large object in that direction.

She gave the command to assume battle stations and ordered the navigator to assume the random tumble. She ordered all weapons personnel to follow the Rope-a-Dope protocol. She then ordered the ship to achieve the speed at which the ship could generate maximum power while still being able to turn and change directions quickly. It was the speed that the four captains had demonstrated with the crew that allowed them to maintain the Javelin's top performance. Non-the-less to an onlooker the tumble while flying through space appeared like a duck shot out of the sky and falling randomly to the ground. It was just not what one would expect and it amazed the observer that the vessel maintained its structural integrity.

Esoteric Journey

On the Bola Satu, Commander Mangkas had his crew at battle stations from the moment the ring of lasers began to fire into the sphere in space that they had formed. His chief battle officer and team had identified that each laser's target was a small particle of dust that was located inside the sphere that had been set up. They commented that it seemed to be a cleaning operation and it demonstrated a high degree of technology and laser accuracy.

When all the lasers pointed at the Bola Satu he again asked what that meant. The Chief battle officer shook her head and said that it was a clear indication that whoever controlled the laser's knew that the Bola Satu was monitoring the area and knew its exact location.

Suddenly the cameras monitoring the area displayed the figure of a very large missile like spaceship appear at the center of the sphere formed by the lasers. It tumbled randomly through, and it appeared to be out of control. He ordered the Bola Satu to follow and to be prepared to shoot. He knew that the Bola Satu was superior to any spaceship that was shaped like a missile. The alien ship was clearly of an ancient design and at the moment it was clearly out of control. His chief battle officer asked whether she should have her missile operators destroy the vessel.

In conference with the leaders on Keterubah he was given permission to fire once the ship stopped. Mangkas decide to keep pace with the vessel. He quickly learned that the Bola Satu was at is maneuverability limits which made him wonder about the survivability of the aliens in the missile shaped vessel.

14 Meeting of the Minds

If Commander Mangkas could have looked in, he would have found Samantha comfortably sitting at her control station monitoring the sphere that was following the Javelin. She had continued the random, tumbling flight while Elisha used her skills to hack into the control system of the sphere.

Elisha was humming to herself as she put back door after back door code into what she considered a naked computer system on the ship. She found a path to the computers on the planet where she was facing a more sophisticated firewall. She gave her thumbs up to Samantha when she had control of the ship.

Samantha called for a stop to their travels, with the Javelin facing the sphere.

Mangkas was surprised when suddenly the tumbling alien spaceship stopped and faced the Bola Satu. The suddenness alarmed him and he ordered his Chief Battle officer to shoot.

She fired one of the more powerful missiles that was destroyed almost immediately.

Samantha was surprised by having a missile fired at them. She had one of the laser operators take the missile out. She in turn order a missile to be fired and to explode near the sphere.

Mangkas was about to order another missile to be fired when a missile exploded almost immediately in front of the control room. He realized that he was facing aliens who were not afraid of a face off and who had weapons as powerful or perhaps more powerful than his.

At almost the same moment his communication officer said that he had a visual that would make him wonder who they were calling aliens. He looked up at the screen and saw a person who could have been any male on the Bola Satu holding up an open empty hand. He almost burst out laughing because it was the first time that his lessons in history had made a difference. He understood the visual because he had seen it in a painting that the lecturer had discussed that showed two ancient armies that were facing each other. In the painting the two leaders were walking toward each other with raised hands empty of weapons. He recalled the lecturer stating the fact that they were not necessarily friends but they were for the moment not a threat to each other.

Elisha gave out a whoop and said that she needed Tom's, Linda's and H^3 help to decipher what she had just discovered as she hacked into the planets computer network system. She pointed to what appeared to be a head set that showed people putting it on and talking with each other. She was not sure that talking was the right description but it was clear to her that they were somehow communicating.

H^3 was the one that said that he thought it was a language translator that read the mind and did the translation at the brain interface level bypassing the need for translation.

14 Meeting of the Minds

Tom said that they had all the equipment to produce such a unit in a matter of a few minutes and rushed to the electronics lab. It took him more than a few minutes but less than two hours later he returned with two electrodes that could be put on the forehead and the back of the neck and translation was directly done by the brain.

He had Samantha put one on and had Yara put another one on. He asked Yara to speak Portuguese and Samantha to speak in Vietnamese and carry on a conversation about how wonderful he was. That had both of them laughing but as they each spoke in their own language; their eyes grew big because the translation was happening.

Joe shook his head as he watched. Tom and Linda had invented the Door which had cured his cancer and had opened up travel across the Universe. They had invented the Hole generator with H^3's help and had opened the universe for the travels they were on. Now Tom had been able to almost immediately create the situation where communication between people, each speaking their own language could understand each other.

He had one of the units mounted on himself and asked that Lydia put on the other. He then had communication established with the leader of the Sphere that was facing the Javelin.

Mangkas had been patiently waiting as the two ships faced each other. He wondered what the next step was to be when the communication appeared to be hampered by the inability of his linguistic officer to understand the communication that they were receiving.

Then he was given one of the new translation caps that had just been issued to his staff. He personally had not found it necessary since everyone spoke the major language of Keterubah.

He looked at the two people comfortably sitting in a room that was decorated with a large ocean scene painting similar to a small one he had in his onboard room. Suddenly he could understand what they were saying.

He smiled when he realized that they were greeting him and asking how his day was going and if he was ready to relax since they were not interested in engaging him in battle. He realized that the male was referred to as Joe and the female as Lydia and that they were a pair.

He also realized that they knew his name and were asking about his wife, Bini, and his young son, Nambelas. He was a bit dazed as they shared some casual dialogue and suggested that they begin the process of getting to know each other in the context of two worlds coming together to understand two worlds of peoples that were from the same roots but who had grown up in worlds separated by multiple galaxies.

He sat in wonder as he realized that the stories about the origin of the people on Keterubah had more truth to them than he had ever been willing to believe. He knew he would have to rethink many of the facts that he thought he knew. He was also amazed that they would have that same technology that had just been developed on Keterubah.

14 Meeting of the Minds

Joe ended the discussion with Mangkas, the commander of the Bola Satu. He then assigned a team to work with Elisha so they could have all the details possible that could be gleaned from the computers they had access to.

He also ordered the team to produce more of the translator units and to get that information back to Jorge and Jerry so they could produce more sophisticated units and get them out to all Cosmos personnel and to the planets that had so far been discovered. He realized that the translation units might end up being the most powerful technology in accelerating the establishment of an Intergalactic community. He knew that being able to communicate with each other was the most important capability people had.

15

Reawakening After Destruction

When the Admiral arrived at the seventh Planet he found what could happen when planetary battles reached a point where the civilization that had risen to amazing heights and unchecked power collided. The collision destroys the very foundation that allowed the prosperity. What the Admiral found and then chose to deal with showed the true nature of his mantra of, "treat others as you wish to be treated." He found a world in desperate need and put together a rescue effort that enrolled the Nivians who he had rescued and empowered them to help a planet that had destroyed itself, the Mirabiro.

It is documented that the Admiral personally purchased every head of cattle available in Earth's market place and had the meat sent to Mirabiro. It is also recorded that four Door modules were put into orbit around Mirabiro to facilitate the deployment of food packages to the survivors that were located along the shores of what essentially was an ash filled ocean. On his arrival, the ash that had spewed into the sky still gave it a grey hue multiple of decades since the devastation of the planet.

15 Reawakening After Destruction

A few survivors were located on the banks of three very large lakes that might have been blue water at some time in the past but were now as grey as the oceans. The grey cast of the whole planet seemed to echo the sadness of a planet that once had wealth and beauty and had been reduced to ash.

During my study of the records dealing with planet seven I discovered mention of Elisha Sands and her fluke discovery of a vault where crystal records of the planets history and the seeds of plants had been stored. It was the planets doomsday vault that held the information and the means to help put the people of Mirabiro on the path to rebuilding their planet. It was the hopes of the past pushing itself into the planets recovery in a devastated future.

The Admiral supported having a team go down to the vault to facilitate its opening, to gain access to the history of Mirabiro and to guide the people to begin the long road of getting the seeds out and planted so they would have a future. From my research I know that this was one of the only times his team made a landing on any of the planets that they had discovered. They risked the exposure to give the people of Mirabiro a chance to have a future.

A final foot note in the record led me to a video that was recovered from a lone satellite that was still orbiting the planet when the Admiral and his team arrived. It had captured the last days of a global battle where missiles seemed to fly in all directions and destroy city after city until finally the sky was so full of ash that the entire planet of Mirabiro was obscured.

It is a soul chilling video that few have watched and very few would ever chose to if they knew what it so graphically showed.

It is also recorded that the Admiral and a team of supporters returned each year to deliver aid to Mirabiro for most of the rest of his life. He is recorded as saying that the galactic human community had benefited in some way from every planet his team had discovered and Mirabiro's contribution was a painful and sad example of why "treating others the way you wish to be treated" was so fundamental and when ignored on a global basis ends in an unimaginable catastrophe.

Again, for me it drives home my feeling that the Admiral was a visionary but he was also a person who had a big heart and wanted to give those around him an opportunity to contribute to the wellbeing of the universe.

****

Before Joe proceeded to the seventh planet he returned to Earth. He was pleased to discover the move to Madorite in the Izulite system in full swing. He knew that the quicker that move occurred the less risk that he and the Cosmos program would face. He also wanted the Intergalactic Association of Worlds to have the opportunity to organize in a manner that gave each world the space to allow it to assume the role it most desired. He desperately did not want to be a conquering explorer.

Jorge let him know that the construction of a facility on the surface of Madorite would house the majority of people on a planet he referred to as the Sahara of worlds but one that had many oasis. Jorge had made the point that the planet had plenty of everything necessary to sustain the number of personnel that would be living there and it turned out that wheat, corn, soybeans, potatoes, and most tropical fruits grew exceedingly well, so food would not be an issue. In fact, he knew that in the near future Madorite would be able to export food.

He added that so far only rabbits, chicken and sheep had been introduced and were also doing well. He made the point that Madorite was eighty percent land mass and only twenty percent water but it turned out that water was actually present almost everywhere just a few feet below a dry surface.

Jerry added that the facilities to process the iron ore and produce the quality of stainless steel that he was using to produce the spheres had been found and was being processed using a small mill mentality that produced the steel on an as needed to order basis. The tools and equipment needed to produce the spherical space craft had been transferred from Earth to Madorite and had been installed in buildings designed for them. The ground production facility was fully functional and staffed.

Final assembly was done in space and followed the concept of the Russian Matryoshka dolls. The smallest of the spheres was sent up and assembled first, then the second, third, fourth and fifth sphere layers were sent up and assembled around the smaller ones.

Each sphere was a single layer except for the exterior sandwich layer that had a water layer to provide radiation shielding. The shield generation units were then attached to the outside and finally the entire sphere was covered in what the engineers were calling shielding foam. The building process was nearing completion of the first sphere that would be ready in time for the ninth planet visit.

Jerry then smiled and said that it would be ready unless like every other trip a new technical specification was added to the vessel.

Jorge let him know that all the Cosmos ships had orbit positions assigned around Madorite and there were no more ships in orbit around Earth. He had heard from President Lebak that the absence of the Cosmos ships had not made any news and the removal of all references of financial support for the Cosmos program that could be legally erased had been done. Jorge then smiled and said that the Presidential elections would soon be occurring and the President had indicated that he was ready to become a part of the Cosmos program.

Joe smiled and said that he was going to designate the Cosmos Javelin as the official diplomatic ship to be used by the President in setting up the United Intergalactic Worlds Organization. He wanted the more advanced Spherical ships to be used for the continued exploration of the Universe.

He asked if the Door building at Lakland would be maintained.

Jorge let him know that Lakland would remain as a fully functioning Cosmos site but its funding would now be handled by the Cosmos program.

Joe nodded and said that he would like to put in several private Doors in locations spread around Earth. He smiled and said that one location would be at his ranch. He suggested that a second one be at Jorge's parents' home in Mexico, another Door should be in Brazil near Yara's parents' home, one in Vermont at Samantha's home and one in England near Tom and Linda's home. He was sure there would be other locations but that would be sufficient to allow he and the crew members of the Cosmos ships to be able to take vacations back on Earth.

He added that eventually strategically positioned Door units would likely serve as vacation avenues for people of the nine worlds to visit each other. He personally envisioned people setting goals to visit all nine planets on their personal vacations.

In the next meeting Joe had with his four captains, Yara asked about the timing for their trip through the Hole. Joe replied that it was up to the four of them. He was ready immediately since they did not have to practice with new technology. The mental communication units had been quickly developed. They had to learn to use them so they could feel comfortable using them.

Samantha suggested that they practice the use of mental communication during their upcoming journey through the Hole. She thought that it might give them an edge when they were randomly maneuvering through space and needing to executed the more difficult tasks of targeting and flying.

Joe agreed and said that they should see if it made any significant difference.

He then suggested they announce the time for the next journey through the Hole.

Tom, Linda and H³ said they had the coordinates for the seventh human colony programed and it was a go for them.

Lacey was the Captain at the helm and gave the order to create the next Hole. She then followed the normal protocol and had the cleaning lasers go through. For once the laser warning lights all stayed green. She ordered the Javelin forward and it held position while Tom began to search for the human populated planet.

Tom was silent for quite some time before he announced that he had identified the planet that was populated by intelligent life. He shook his head as he continued and added that it appeared that there had been some sort of major conflict and he was not sure how many humans were still alive on a very devastated third planet. He put the video of what the three search telescopes on the Javelin could make out. The sky was grey, what appeared to be three separate oceans were all grey, and the land was grey. There were major ruins spread around the planet. Tom used a laser pointer to point to about half a dozen locations where it appeared humans were gathered and seemed to be eking out a survival style of living. He continued and said that given what he had so far been able of find it appeared that the global population was down to perhaps a million individuals. He went on to say that the ruins of the cities that were around the planet would indicate that at one time some six billion people had populated the planet.

15 Reawakening After Destruction

There was total silence as Joe took in the magnitude of destruction.

He asked Tom where the biggest group of survivors were located.

H^3 replied that he had done that survey and found that there were three groups that seemed to number in the thousands and then there were numerous smaller groups spread randomly around the planet.

Yara and Samantha both seemed to ask the same question at the same time. "What should we do to help?"

Joe shook his head. He said that he was going to break the rule that they had set up about not interfering with a planets social order. He looked around and said that they had gained tremendous knowledge and technology from the other worlds that they had visited. This time it was their turn to see how they could help get this planet on a journey up from the depths that they were currently in.

He said that their quest to find all nine planets would take a pause so they could get this planet on a path to recovery while there was still the opportunity to do so.

Lydia suggested that they recruit several key people that were knowledgeable on how to provide the aid required by people experiencing a major catastrophe.

Joe agreed and suggested they get Jorge to do that recruiting. He then said that they should prepare a way for that aid to get to the people needing it. A first step would be to establish communication with the leaders of the three largest groups and see what immediate help they needed.

Darian agreed that was a great first step but those three groups only represented about thirty thousand people out of the million or so that were hanging on to life. He wanted to immediately drop food, shelter, and clothing to all the rest as well. He suggested they strategically locate orbiting Doors that could drop supplies down to all the survivors.

Joe said that was a great suggestion and they would do that immediately. They didn't need to be precise about giving aid they just needed to be giving aid in time. He suggested getting the Doors launched immediately. He would make sure there was food to be sent down by buying it on Earth and having it sent continuously to each of the doors where it could be organized and sent down to the planet via parachutes.

On the surface of Mirabiro, Ngati sat shivering in the make shift structure that housed a dozen of the survivors. He knew that they were not really survivors, they were just the ones too stubborn to die. He and a significant number of other persons too stubborn to die had found a source of food that was keeping roughly ten thousand people from dying. They had food but the cold was slowly taking the weaker people. He wondered if there were other groups around Mirabiro that had survived. He hoped so. He hoped that they were doing better than the group he was leading. He knew that unless there was a miracle the Mirabiroans were doomed and would soon cease to exist. The arrogance of those in power had led to the total destruction of a population of close to five billion on the verge of being able to sustain a wonderful life on a gorgeous planet.

He was suddenly pulled out of his thoughts when one of his followers said that something strange was happening and he needed to come out and look up into the sky.

Ngati walked out and looked up to where his follower was pointing. He could barely see through the grey of the polluted sky but it was clear that something was above and was blinking a red light. He wondered what country had been able to recover and launch a satellite. Suddenly he saw a huge box coming down on a huge parachute. The box landed very close to where he was standing. The parachute was larger than any he had ever seen. His immediate reaction was that it would make a shelter better than the one he and his closest followers had. He had a team surround the box and also recover the parachute. It alone would make a huge difference in how they all slept that night.

He approached the box and smiled as he saw that a crowbar had been provided to enable opening the box. He gave instructions to keep the box and the material in as good of a shape as possible. It was almost as valuable as the parachute.

There was also a smaller box attached to the huge container box. He walked up to it. It had a small handle that when he turned it opened the box. Inside was what appeared to be a gamers headset. He almost laughed when he saw it but then decided that he should put it on.

When he did the world took on a new meaning. He suddenly realized he was in contact with someone who seemed to be talking to him.

He heard someone greeting him and offering to help in any way possible. Tears were in his eyes as he hugged Dhako his wife and his daughter, Nyathin. He had no idea how the headset worked but he knew he was communicating with a person called Joe who explained that he and his team were going to help. The box contained warm clothing, thermal shelters, and food that would help feed the ten thousand people that were located around him. This Joe let him know that a constant supply would be delivered until food could be grown by those on the planet. He almost stumbled as he tried to find a place to sit down. What he was feeling was a euphoria that was intoxicating. The grey world around him had suddenly burst into color.

Joe asked him to share what the star, the collection of planets were called and what he preferred to be called.

He realized that as Joe asked for information his mind was providing it. He smiled and hoped that Joe would not ask anything personal.

He asked Joe what country had been able to survive the war. That was when his world once again seemed to explode as he learned that there were no surviving countries and that all of Mirabiro was a grey world.

He was about to ask where Joe came from when suddenly he saw a planet similar to what Mirabiro had looked like before the war and learned that Joe came from across the universe from a planet called Earth.

15 Reawakening After Destruction

It was hard for Ngati to absorb but at the moment he did not have the energy to question where Joe was from. He needed the food and especially the warm clothes that he saw as the large crate was opened.

Joe let him know that he should put on the headset each day and he would be in conversation with a person that would be arranging how to guide him on getting the people he was leading back on their feet and once again able to feed themselves.

Joe got off the first of several similar sessions with the leaders of the surviving groups that were spread around Mirabiro. He ended up having eight Doors orbiting the planet and supplies being dropped on a daily basis. He had no illusions about the amount of aid and effort it would take to get the Mirabirons back on their feet and able to take care of themselves.

He also knew that the Cosmos program had the network, financial resources, and the ability to support Mirabiro through the countless years that it would take to bring it back to a green surviving world.

16

Greening of Mirabiro

I was pleasantly surprised by finding more detail on what the Admiral and his team did after they discovered the devastated seventh colony. It made my day to find that account. It truly cements the admiration I have for the Admiral. The fact that getting the survivors of the seventh planet back on track to live well and to live in harmony with each other became a focus for his team speaks volumes to the character of he and his team. Not only do records show that the actions taken were immediate and got the planet close to normal in a short time but I have visited the seventh human colony and was amazed that turning grey dust into bright green, creating a planet that was a blooming dazzling multicolored flower of beauty was possible. What was very impressive was that the transition was handled in a fashion that allowed for immediate aid to literally come down from the sky via huge parachutes that delivered food and other necessities but the parachutes themselves were designed to be converted into large shelters.

16 Greening of Mirabiro

I dug through all the records to get detailed information about the multiple dust collectors that collected the dust and produced grey bricks. The grey bricks in turn became the foundation for the many structures that were build. The removal of dust continues to this day and are turned into useful items like boat hulls, posts, and floor coverings. It has even been used as base material for the train tracks in the tunnels that connect the six new cities located around the planet. Dust, to bricks to train tracks connecting a once again thriving world; the transformation made possible by a visionary, the Admiral that I have come to admire.

The Admiral is also credited with guiding the political structure that rules Mirabiro. He facilitated bringing the survivors of the various fighting factions together to form one world governing body. This created a unifying attitude that has served to create a world at peace. It is seen as a political structure that has the framework that will stand the test of time.

What is also very inspiring is the fact the planet was turned green based on utilizing the seeds and the DNA of various species of animals found in a doomsday vault to bring back what was lost in the devastation of the fruitless war that was fought. The Admiral's team found the doomsday vault that had been used to store the seeds, and the DNA that would allow the devastated world a chance to recover. It opened that vault and guided the people of the seventh colony to the recovery that is still going on to this day.

The Admiral commissioned a memorial that features a series of hour long videos that show how the planet was devastated piece by piece until there was nothing left. It is by far the most famous of a host of memorials that have been built on Mirabiro.

The record shows that the Cosmos Javelin remained in orbit around Mirabiro for several years. During that time, its function and purpose was transitioned to become the headquarters for the formation of the Intergalactic Association of Worlds. Mirabiro became one of the first to accept membership. It was too early for them to be cleared to be present physically but they had a seat at the table and input to how the organization would function. Their representative was one of the first to support the inclusion of the Intergalactic Space Force that was led by the Admiral. Their representatives consistently supported anything that the Admiral suggested. The Admiral is by far the most well-known, admired, and revered person on Mirabiro. There are also many Mirabiro heroes and heroines but they all credited the Admiral for having saved their world.

****

Joe had spent most of the week communicating with various leaders on the surface of Mirabiro. It was clear to him that it was going to take much more than his team to guide the recovery of the planet. He asked Lydia and Lacey to work together to arrange for the consistent support supplies that would be needed. He asked that they make sure that the aid was prioritized to fit the needs of each group. He was sure that food and shelter would be a priority.

16 Greening of Mirabiro

Elisha excitedly reported that she had been looking for any source of a working computer or electronic system and had found two sources. One was a lone satellite in a seriously decaying orbit whose control computer she had been able to hack into and a very weak source that seemed to be a computer control system for some sort of massive structure that seemed to be intact.

Joe assigned Tom and H^3 to looked into the structure. He wanted to know what it might be.

Tom was looking at the structure through the ships three telescopes and when he filtered out the obstructing grey of the dust, Linda shouted out that it was a Doomsday vault and it looked like it had survived the planets Doomsday.

Joe listened to the three who said that they would need to go to the surface to see if they could open it. Joe shook his head and replied that was not how it would happen. He asked which of the groups that they had made contact with was the closest to the structure.

It turned out that the individual that he knew as Ngati was. He spent time discussing the situation with him and that the Doomsday building would most likely hold all the seeds and DNA of the animals that had populated Mirabiro. He pointed out that what was needed was to have fertile ground and the water to grow the plants. Joe let him know that what each of the groups spread around the planet needed to do was to clear the dust from the ground and the fresh water sources.

Once he had communicated a similar message to all the other major group leaders he contacted meteorological experts on Earth and asked them to recommend how a planet that was encased in a layer of dust in the atmosphere, the land and the ocean could clean itself.

He learned that the first step would be to seed the atmosphere to cause rain that would effectively wash the dust from the air and deliver it to the ground. The rain would also cause much of the dust on the ground to be washed to the lower levels of the land, down rivers and to the ocean. However, the density of the dust might mean that it would embed itself in the streams and settle to the bottom of the ocean. The experts pointed out that cleaning the streams, rivers and oceans would take centuries.

Joe let Jorge and Jerry who now resided on Madorite about the situation. They agreed to take over the relief effort. They would staff it for the long term and move as fast as they could in getting the Mirabiro planet on a path to total recovery.

Jerry let Joe know that the first of the spherical Cosmos Spaceships was ready for commissioning.

Joe struggled to think of a name that he wanted to name the new vessel. He asked Lydia, Lacey, Samantha and Yara what they thought their first spherical Cosmos ship should be named.

Samantha suggested they keep the naming simple and name the first spherical Cosmos spacecraft USS Cosmos Sphere One. Then subsequent ships could be given the same family name and a number to designate when it was added to the fleet.

Lydia said that the USS should be dropped and instead the designation for all of the Cosmos Fleet should be ISF made up of the first letters of the Intergalactic Space Force. So, she added, their new ship should be named ISF Cosmos Sphere One.

Joe listened as the four took a circuitous route through the languages to see if there was a better name using the different languages of Europe and Asia. After about an hour he called a halt to the naming game and declared that ISF Cosmos Sphere One would be what he would ask the new leader of the United Intergalactic World Organization (UIWO) to Christen the new ship.

Lacey smiled and asked when her successor was taking the helm of the UIWO.

Joe returned her smile and said that he was now on his way and would take over command of the renamed ISF Javelin on the following day. The day after that, he and the four of them would transit to the ISF Cosmos Sphere One.

Yara chuckled and added that then they would practice, practice and practice until the fat lady sang and then practice some more.

Samantha shook her head and added that they had two more planets to visit to complete their current extended journey and they would be facing the two planets that had been in existence the longest of all. Their next jump would take them another one hundred thousand years into technology that they had no clue about.

Lydia nodded and said that she hoped that what they were challenged by was something that they could overcome but nothing like what they had found had occurred on the seventh planet. It was for her the finding of the planet of doom. She hoped that in her life time she would be able to come back and visit Mirabiro and walk through green valleys that sported wild flowers and whatever small animals once lived there.

The next day the five of them met with ex-President Lebak who insisted they now call him Craig. They explained the name changes that they proposed for the entire fleet and the name of the new ship that they were asking him to commission. Craig thanked them for giving him the honor to rename all the ships and to Christen the new spherical ship.

Joe let him know that he would have control of the ISF Javelin and should staff it the way that he wanted because they were taking all the operational personnel currently serving on it with them to their new ship. Joe smiled and said that it was not going to be difficult to get qualified personnel and he should get in contact with Rear Admiral Jorge Martinez, or Jorge as he liked to be called and arrange for the Javelin to get staffed.

Craig chuckled and said that he would need to get use to the speed at which events around ISF took place so he could keep up.

When he learned why the ISF Javelin had remained in place for more than a year and that it was scheduled to stay there for however long it took to get the seventh colony and the planet back to an upward trajectory and he learned of the current situation, he said that he would do his best to make it happen in their life time.

Joe nodded and said that he would be returning to see what had been accomplished when they made it to seeding planet nine.

17

Eighth Colony Challenge

As I report on the Admirals continuing journey I am amazed that he and his crew survived the assault that he, his crew, and the new ship faced as they entered into the region of space where the eighth seeded planet of Kelapan existed in the Sulwe system. The assault was recorded as having been led by a very nervous Commander Keadilan who had just barely survived a battle with an alien fighting group that had crossed the distance from a nearby star and demanded the Kelapan people capitulate to them and pay them in a variety of minerals. His ship was newly commissioned and he and his inexperience crew put up a courageous battle and were able to drive the alien group away. However, they had taken a beating that had required significant repairs and cost the lives of ten of the crew. They were on watch for the return of the aliens when the appearance of the Cosmos Terra cleaning lasers came through and began cleaning out the particles in the Sphere's transit area. This was taken as a display of power that caused Commander Keadilan to take immediate action to counter and he ordered their destruction.

17 Eighth Colony Challenge

The historical records show that this was one time that the Admiral chose not to come through the initial Hole but requested a second Hole located away from the first. The change in location gave the Admiral the ability to enter the solar system and immediately send a signal of friendship.

This was received but not believed and instead Commander Kelapan chose to fire directly at the Admiral's ship.

Then from what I was able to learn from the records the Admiral ordered the Cosmos Sphere to eliminate the powerful laser that had hit the Sphere and rocked it to the core. This happened two more times until the Cosmos Sphere had eliminated all the lasers that had fired on it. Throughout the face off, records show that the Admiral repeatedly sent out the message indicating friendship.

Records also tell of the crew testing to see if the much larger sphere that they were facing had shielding that would prevent their missiles from destroying it. They learned that it did not. Additionally, the Cosmos Terra's supreme hacker, Elisha Sands is said to have gained access to the control system on the Kelapan ship.

The Admiral once again sent the picture of his empty hand raised and at the same time had the lights in the Kelapan ship blink on and off several times in rhythm with his picture blinking. I find this somewhat amusing but what is written indicates that Commander Keadilan was stunned and tried to fire all weapons. They had all been disabled and the confrontation finally subsided when he realized he no longer controlled his own ship.

Again, I sit at my work consol in admiration of how the Admiral dealt with what turned out to be a very frightened Kelapan leadership. What I almost missed was that the Admiral took the additional action of paying a visit to the aliens that had threatened the eighth human planet. That venture turned out to be a story of its own.

****

Joe and the entire crew transited directly to the ISF Cosmos Sphere One and moved into what would be their primary fleet ship. It was clear to all of them that they had stepped up in class and spaciousness. Joe smiled when he entered his and Lydia's personal quarters and there was a bouquet of roses for Lydia. He wondered who had thought of that touch. Later he learned that the roses had been sent by Uncle Ted, who had become an avid follower of what was transpiring on the Esoteric journey. He also learned that Uncle Ted's source of information was none other than one of his Chef students.

Fabio the current Chef for the Cosmos Sphere toured the new kitchen with his staff of two. They were admiring their new kingdom. They were all looking over the cooking area as well as the area where the crew would be enjoying their meals. Fabio picked up a package with his name on it and a picture of the ranch. He knew that his teacher, Uncle Ted had sent him something special. He opened it to find three seasoned perfectly marbled ribeye steaks and three bacon wrapped filet mignon. He smiled and read the card that thanked him for, "being the perfect informant" and hoped he and his team enjoyed the steaks.

17 Eighth Colony Challenge

Uncle Ted and Trey sat on the veranda and watched the construction of the extension to the barn. It was being prepared to house a Door unit. They were also aware of the work to bring in a second power line to provide the power for the Door. Both of them were looking forward to being able to have Joe and Lydia return at any time for visits. They also agreed that they would learn to use the door and begin exploring the universe while they were still able. Both of them were in agreement that this ability would take them where they had never dreamt of ever going. It would be a way that they could see what Joe had been up to.

What Joe was up to was taking the Cosmos Sphere through every exercise that the four captains and he had put together. This time the practice ended sooner than before because the crew was experienced and that Sphere performed flawlessly. The new headsets allowing the crew to communicate mind to mind was tested and proved to greatly improve everyone's performance.

Joe learned that the Door to the ranch had been installed and was ready for use. He invited the leadership team to the ranch and announced a one day liberty for everyone. He was ready for some fishing and a ride across the ranch.

When he and Lydia came out of the Door receiving "shed" Joe stepped back and scanned the extension that had been added to the barn. The building had been blended into the barn in such a fashion that it looked like an original part. He was impressed with the work.

The power lines that he knew had been brought in from more than ten miles away were also blended in and looked as if they had always been there. The Door when used drew as much power as the ranch did in a month.

This visit was a good test since his entire leadership team had taken him up on visiting the ranch. He and Lydia walked up to the house where his father was waiting for them. They let him know that it was going to be a busy couple of days on the ranch since most of the team was going to be showing up that day.

Uncle Ted came out and after hugs and greetings, he asked when he and Trey could get a lesson on how to use the new contraption that had disfigured the clean lines of the barn.

Lydia laughed and said that she too felt the clean lines of the barn had been harmed. She pointed to the new red brick sidewalk leading toward the house and commented on the fact that a good part of the lawn had also been lost.

Uncle Ted nodded and said that he hoped to use the Door to go to some beach in the Hawaiian Islands.

Joe shook his head and said that a Door at the ranch was one of the few out in the civilian world. He, however, would be glad to take both he and his dad up to see the new spaceship, ISF Cosmos Sphere One, the had just been commissioned.

Uncle Ted said that would be great and he would be ready after they all enjoyed a great dinner and desert.

17 Eighth Colony Challenge

After the arrival and settling of the team they were all sitting on the veranda watching the shimmering sun slowly descent toward the western horizon. A herd of cattle standing along the top of the hill all appeared to be black silhouettes against clouds being turned yellow on the undersides by the sun's last rays when Uncle Ted called them in for dinner.

Lacey said that she would remember the glorious view during their next confrontation or battle. She then stood up and walked around the veranda to the kitchen entry door. Everyone rose and followed as the grey of night seemed descent with the last sliver of the sun disappearing below the horizon and the cattle seemed to disappear as well.

It was almost immediately after dinner that Uncle Ted said the he was ready for his tour of the new spaceship.

Joe led the way and explained how the Door was used and led the way. His arrival on Sphere One surprised the crew that was on duty. He let them know that they should relax and that he was acting as a tour guide. He arranged for two appropriately sized blue coveralls to be provided and that he had Chef Ted Stratford and the beef supplier Trey Elsinger coming for a tour of the Sphere.

No one seemed to link the two arrivals to him until they got to the first tour stop, the kitchen and mess area. Fabio had chosen to stay on board and get the kitchen organized for the coming journey to the eighth planet. He let out a loud whoop, ran to Uncle Ted, and gave him a hug. He pulled him around the kitchen showing off all the new equipment.

He then led the way to the freezer and opened it to show all the boxes that he had personally labeled with the letters UT or RCH to indicate that it was the beef or other goods that came from the ranch. He introduced Uncle Ted to his two kitchen staff who seemed as star struck as two groupies being able to shake hands with their favorite singing or acting star.

When they got to the control room, Joe put the Izulite star on screen and let them know that they were looking at the equivalent of the sun but the star was called Izulite and the planet that they were orbiting was Madorite the new base for the Cosmos program and where the materials for Sphere One had been mined and processed.

It was then that Uncle Ted realized that he had traveled out of the Solar System and across to a different part of the universe. He asked if travel to all the other planets that Joe had so far visited was as easy.

Joe nodded and said that at the current time the visits would only be to Door's that orbited the planets there, but in the future he could see the planets being visited through Doors that would be located on their surfaces.

His father had been rather quiet and asked why the grand ship that they were visiting was name with such an impersonal name such as Sphere One.

Joe smiled and said that his team had struggled with the name and had finally thrown up their hands when they could not think of a name.

His father nodded and asked why not give each sphere the name of each of the nine planets. That would make the first sphere Earth One or to make it more romantic it could be called Gaia or Terra. The next sphere could be called Nivian after the second human planet found.

Joe smiled and said that when they got back to the ranch he should propose the name change to the four captains that he was sure would be sitting on the veranda sipping wine or drinking a cool one. He added that he personally would be thrown off the veranda if he proposed it.

Uncle Ted laughed and said that he had gone out and bought his first case of Schlitz to make sure Joe would not again complain about being out of it and it would be a shame if he was not allowed to sit on the veranda and enjoy a cold one.

That seemed a good note to end the tour on and the three of them returned to the ranch.

When they got out of the Door unit Uncle Ted asked why everyone had to go through the Door naked.

Joe shook his head and pointed to Tom and Linda who were each holding a bottle of Schlitz and told him to ask the two genius's.

He watched Uncle Ted walk over and knew that Tom would probably have a good yarn to tell.

Early the next morning with the entire team strung out along the creek fishing, Joe gathered the four captains for a few moments and said that his father had suggested that the new ship should be named after the planet they all came from, and the subsequent ships be named after the other eight planets they were visiting. That got an immediate nod of approval and the two names that were discussed was Gaia or Terra.

Samantha said she preferred Terra because it had a double meaning for her. It was the Latin name for the Earth but it was also the name of a Roman goddess and terra firma was often a way to describe dry land. That combination screamed out to her to name the ship "Terra."

Agreement was immediately reached to rename the first spherical space craft ISF Cosmos Terra and the four went back to their fishing.

Joe was left sitting amazed that it had been that easy.

Later after they were all out on the veranda while the fresh trout lunch was being prepared, Joe held a ceremony where their ship was renamed. He thanked his father and poured a small glass of champaign for all of them in celebration.

During their ride across the ranch on La and Tui their two new horses, Lydia commented that she was pleased that they had embraced the name change that his father had suggested because it greatly personalized the new ship for her and she knew that the other three captains liked the new name as well.

Joe nodded and said that he agreed and it provided the basis for naming the ships that would follow.

17 Eighth Colony Challenge

The next morning, they all made the transit to the Cosmos Terra and spent the rest of the day in preparation for their next through the Hole Transit.

The morning after, Joe was sitting at his command station, Yara was the captain that was due to take the ship through the next hole. She issued the command for the Hole creation and then sent through the cleaning lasers. A few moments later they all watched as laser after laser was pulverized. Two of the lasers were able to swing around and show a huge spherical spaceship before they too were eliminated.

Joe asked for coordinates for a hole on the other side of the solar system that would give them time to make the transit through the Hole.

Everyone was aware that this was an unusual move. Joe gave his reasoning as a way to get into a defensive position and not have the very powerful vessel attacking. He did not want to destroy a ship that most likely held the humans that they were out looking for. He ordered all hands to be prepared but to only take the actions that would disable the ship that was attacking.

Once the Terra transited through the Hole, Elisha was scanning the giant sphere as it made its approach across the system they were in. She was feverishly looking for a way to send her hacking patch into any computer like program that she could touch. She had expected a firewall that would prevent her from getting in but was surprised that there was none.

She worked with all the speed possible in locating the control systems for propulsion and for the fire control system. She listened as Joe repeatedly sent messages of friendship only to get the response of a missile fired at the Terra. She heard Yara three times giving the command to destroy the laser.

She finally found the propulsion control system and shut it down. She then found the fire control system and took it off line. She knew that she had just had a great day hacking and let out the cry of Voya!

Yara had defended the Terra by returning fire that took out each of the three giant laser cannons mounted around the sphere that had fired on it. Her gunnery team had verified that the sphere they faced did not have shielding that would prevent them from destroying the ship.

On the Bola, Commander Kelapan had acted immediately to eliminate the alien display of their fire power. He was pleased at the ease with which his laser operators destroyed the smaller lasers that had mysteriously appeared and arranged themselves in a very large sphere. He was informed by his science officer that the firing of the lasers was not a demonstration of fire power but a part of destroying all small particles inside of the sphere they formed. He listened but non-the-less ordered their destruction.

A few moments later a similar action of lasers firing was observed across the Sulwe system he ordered his ship to make a full speed transit to the new location. During the transit he observed a much smaller sphere magically appear at the center of the space formed by what he now knew were cleaning lasers.

He ordered an immediate blast from all three of his laser cannons. He watched in amazement as the lasers hit their target but seemed to have little to no effect.

At the same time, he again received what he took to be a false alien message that signaled the fact that they were friendly. He knew it was a fake message because the picture he was seeing could have been his brother in law. He ordered each of his three giant lasers to fire independently at the smaller alien sphere. He was shocked by the accuracy of responding laser fire as he lost each of the Bola's lasers after they fired. Then the lights dimmed three times and all propulsion was lost.

Then once again the picture of a man holding up his empty hand indicating a desire to be a friend was shown three times as the lights in the Bola dimmed with each showing. It was then he realized that alien or human the smaller sphere now had control of his ship.

He was more amazed when the picture of Sulwe was flashed on the screen with the correct attribution of the Star. Then Kelapan was flashed on the screen with the correct attribution. The his own face was shown with his name, his wife's name and his two children's names were flashed on screen. He was in shock as he tried to comprehend how the aliens could possibly have such detailed information.

This was once again followed by the person holding up his empty hand.

He decided that he had no choice but to reply showing himself holding up his empty hand.

Joe was exceedingly pleased with the information that Elisha was supplying him. She had not stopped once she had disabled the ship but had retrieved the personal information on the Commander Keadilan and his family. Then she had identified his superiors and had followed that path to the entire governmental structure of Kelapan. She had information streaming into their crystalline memory cubes and would in a few hours have the entire history of the planet.

Tom and H^3 were pouring over the design of the huge lasers that had demonstrated power they did not think was possible to achieve. They figured that reverse engineering that capability would be something that the support team back on Madorite would be able to rapidly achieve. They both agreed that the only power greater than the giant lasers was the Hole cannon.

Joe agreed that more powerful lasers was a good find but he identified the fact that three of them combined had not been able to break through the defensive shield that surrounded the Cosmos Terra. He asked Elisha to keep digging to see if they could learn why the Kelapanians had been so aggressive and non-responsive to his repeated signaling of friendship.

17 Eighth Colony Challenge

18

The Jomaoko

This is the almost lost record about the side trip that the Admiral took prior to his visit of the ninth planet. I am of the ninth planet and know well that his arrival here was a pivotal moment for my society. It was a moment that found my world lost and asleep. Once again I ramble and need to refocus on the fact that such a side trip was unusual for the Admiral to make. He did so after learning of the attack by a civilization close enough to transit from one star system to another simply for the desire to conquer and subjugate another civilization.

The Admiral is on record asking Tom, Linda and H^3 to find where that alien civilization resided. He then ordered the Cosmos Terra to transit to a safe distance away from the system of planets that orbited that star.

It is of interest to me that he anticipated a battle and still chose to confront the aliens. His actions clearly demonstrate to me a tremendous confidence he had in his ship and in the crew that made it function. He knew that the performance of his people was what made the Cosmos Terra close to invincible.

18 The Jomaoko

What is of even more wonder to me is that the aliens that he faced were very confident in their ability to overcome what they took to be an insignificant alien vessel with their fleet of star traveling warships. It is safe to say that sixty space going vessels is a fleet. Had they known of the Admiral's experience fighting the Swarm they might had thought twice about attacking him, but they did not have that knowledge. Had they known about his defeating the Invictus with its almost impregnable shield they would not have initiated an attack. But it is clear from the historical records that they did not know, and they unleashed their fleet to eliminate the alien sphere.

The Admiral and his team took the aliens for a Rope-a-dope ride that swiftly depleted their fleet and in the end left the planet open to reprisal. But of course, assimilation, not reprisal was what the Admiral had in mind. He won his battles, but he always had his eye on peace.

The Admiral's team used all their resources and by the time they delivered their Rope-a-dope ending performance they had the information and the access to the alien's global communication and information systems that put them in control. It was at this point in time that the neural headset gave them another breakthrough capability. They could read the alien script based on their minds doing neural translations.

Esoteric Journey

I found that Elisha was able to penetrate the neural network and work her magic. She captured its history, the technical capabilities and was able to utilize the neural headset to translate all the material, organize it and put it on the organic crystalline information storage cubes.

One of the weapons that the aliens had was a weapon capable of penetrating the first layer of the Terra's defensive shield. This was a weapon that was totally, "alien" to Tom and H^3 who found the prints to it in the neural network. They immediately sent that information back to the engineering support team on Madorite asking them to reverse engineer the weapon for use by the Cosmos Terra.

The Admiral took note of his team's ability to penetrate the alien information system. He found it very interesting how close evolution on the alien planet had been to what had taken place on the other alien planets that his team had so far discovered. These aliens could have been cousins of the Draconians that the team had likened to dinosaurs that had evolved and were intelligent. The key difference seems to have been the fact that that Draconians had dark brown scales and the Jomaokoans had a smooth green hide.

This ends my description of the Admirals visit to the Jomaokoans and I eagerly looked forward to my research on his visit to the ninth world. It is my world and what I learned while doing the research on the Admiral opened my eyes, my mind, and my soul to what my planet had accomplished and then slowly lost. It is a feeling that now flows through me on a daily basis.

****

18 The Jomaoko

Joe quickly recognized that Kelapan was a society recovering from having faced an unexpected attack on their planet. He thought of it as the deer frozen in the middle of the road as the headlights blinded it. Like the deer they did not know how to act. They had the technology to defend themselves. They had anticipated and prepared to go out and look for intelligent beings. Instead, unexpectedly they had been faced with a very antagonistic invasion of aliens desiring to conquer and dominate. He found it hard to understand but his experience with the Rilagan and their sentinel ship Invictus that had destroyed the Odessey gave him the basis to understand how a planet with the powerful ship that he had just incapacitated was cowering in fear of facing an alien enemy.

He once again reached out and asked Tom, Linda and H^3, the three persons who he considered his hunters and discoverers, to find the star system close enough to travel to Sulwe in a timely manner.

In short order they had pinpointed a star near enough that conventional travel at half the speed of light would allow a fleet of ships to transit to Sulwe and wage an attack. They calculated the coordinates for the Hole that would put them in the middle of the planets orbiting that star.

Joe put two Door modules in orbit around Kelapan and left them staffed so they could establish solid relationships with the Kelapanians. He made sure that the leader there understood that he and the Cosmos Terra were going to pay a visit to the aliens that had attacked them.

Commander Keadilan of the spherical Kelapan spaceship was impressed that the leader of the vessel that he had attacked was going to take the fight to the aliens that had terrorized Kelapan. He personally wished that he could accompany him, but his ship was currently under repair, and it was clear that he did not enjoy the use of a technology that seemed to defy the law of physics that he knew. He stood and watched as the sphere that he had learned was called the Cosmos Terra disappeared from the sky.

On the other side of the Hole, Dainoso, watched as a sphere of lasers fired inwardly for some mysterious reason and then suddenly a sphere appeared at the center and rotated slowly as if looking for something. Dainoso commanded his fleet to move into position to engage. He contacted command to let them know about the mysterious appearance of the sphere to see what they would want to do.

Lydia took the Terra through in battle ready status and immediately turned to face the fleet of ships that was speeding toward it. She had alerted her laser operators to be ready to respond to any attack with standing orders to hit the offending vessel direct at its forward section. She noted that the spaceships were shaped more like a five sided star fruit when one looked at them on end. It seemed to have missiles nestled in each of the five grooves and lasers mounted out on the top edges. The ship appeared to be designed to fight head on battles. She thought about the lasers mounted on the Terra that were designed to fire in any direction and could do so while the Terra was spinning or weaving.

18 The Jomaoko

Tom, Linda and H^3 scanned the planets and determined that two of them were in the goldilocks zone and a third was evidently being exploited for its minerals. However, all three planets appeared stressed and polluted. It appeared that only one planet was populated by a dense population. The other planet in the goldilocks zone appeared to be a dry planet that was being stripped of its resources as indicated by a thick pollution layer of what were effluents from chemical factories, foundries, and steel mills and what might be oil refineries. A similar situation existed on the planet outside of the goldilocks zone but clearly a planet that was also suffering under the weight of extreme pollution. They commented that it was no wonder that the beings in this system were looking to exploit the planets in the Sulwe system.

The planet populated by a relatively high number of population centers was the one in the goldilocks zone closest to the star. There were three other planets between it and the star.

Elisha had, as was now her role, been trying to get into the control systems of the fleet of ships that surrounded them. She was faced with the fact that the technology she was trying to access was very different in nature from the technology that she had been so successful in getting into in the past. She tried utilizing the neural technology that had allowed her recently to open up the entire history of human planet number eight. In the current situation what she opened up was a strange world of symbols and swirls.

Instead of trying to gather and organize information she concluded that she should instead see if she could gum up the functioning of what she knew was a computer program in a language that was indeed alien to her. She put in lines of code that replicated itself if it was challenged by code trying to shut it down. It was immediately attacked by and began its self-replication as its defense mechanism. She knew it was a only a matter of time before her routine ate up all the computing space in the alien computer.

Tom focused his efforts on identifying missile launch sites that might be on any of the three planets. It did not surprise him to find most of them on the planet that was outside of the goldilocks zone.

As Joe took in the information that was streaming in about what they were facing he sent out his usual empty raised hand in an initial attempt to avoid confrontation.

Dainoso stood at his control station monitoring the arrival of a sphere shaped vessel that had a symbol, IFT COSMOS TERRA, which went halfway around it. He figured it was the name given to the sphere that he had in the bulls eye of his fleets' weapons. He was ready to annihilate the beings that he anticipated were in the spaceship and was only waiting for his leaders on the surface to let loose of the restraints they had over him.

Joe had the picture of him holding his hand up as he sought to establish contact reached the fleet of ships that were making their way toward him.

18 The Jomaoko

It was clear that the ships approaching were spread out like a three dimensional armada use to attacking in a spread formation that reminded him of looking down into the caldera of a volcano. He noted that at the depth of the apparent caldera it seemed to end with three ships that formed some sort of unified weapon. He asked Tom to take a close look and let him know what he saw.

Tom aimed multiple telescopes at the advancing alien formation. He replied that it appeared that it was some sort of huge weapon.

Joe ordered a dense screen of Sparrow projectiles to be launched to shield the Terra from whatever the weapon was designed to do.

He asked Elisha to see if she could get into the control system of the three vessels in the depth of the cone formed by the oncoming ships.

Elisha asked H^3 to give her a hand because she recognized that he had an uncanny way of interacting with code that actually mirrored hers. She hoped that between the two of them they could figure out how to create some havoc.

H^3 let Elisha place the back door into the alien code and then he put the routine he liked to use. It was not intended to do much more than to replicated and fill memory space. It had proved to be an excellent way to rapidly disrupt any computer operation. His routine began the process of round robin partitioning of the data set in a computer. It created a node, pushed data its way, then created as second node and pushed data that way. It kept doing so until it was told there was no room for the last node then it began over again with the first node.

It was a round robin routine that portioned in a combination of both horizontal and vertical nodes until all available space was used up. He especially liked it because during the process any control system counting on it for direction became spasmatic and randomly did what it was intended to do until it ceased to function.

Dainoso received the video of the alien foolishly holding up and empty hand. He received it and the authorization to eliminate the alien ship at the same time. He decided to use his primary weapon that had been developed to be used as a planet killer and was housed in three missiles that were at the center of the fleet. He ordered the sphere to be destroyed. He was sure that it would all be over as soon as he fired the Janekmar. It had been developed for the return of the fleet to the star system where they had met the resistance of a very well-armed planet and was intended to flatten the entire planet and destroy anything that stood in the way of Jomaoko taking possession of the planets in that system. He had personally use the Janekmar and had destroyed two planet sized asteroids.

He gave the order to destroy the sphere and had his Janekmar operator fire the weapon. The Janekmar fired but rather than send out its destructive ray in a tight beam at the sphere the ray left the aiming dish in a swirling pattern that striped every vessel that formed the cone in front of it of its hull. In an instant he lost the twelve ships that formed that cone and the Janekmar could not be turned off. It was destined to keep firing until it used all of the fuel used to power it. It's firing was out of control and destroying his own ships.

18 The Jomaoko

Joe watched as H^3 and Elisha high fived and then jumped up and down shouting, "Voya…Voya…Voya." It was clear that the destruction of the entire cone that went back to whatever the weapon that was now spontaneously firing and destroying all the battle ships that formed the depression cone was the work of the two.

Then he saw all the lasers on all the ships fire simultaneously toward the Terra.

He watched as Lydia had the Terra dancing randomly and moving toward the oncoming fleet while firing every Sparrow system and having their long range missiles taking out many of the lasers that were firing at them.

In a state of disbelief, Dainoso ordered all ships and all weapons to fire on the sphere. He was sure that his team would soon destroy the sphere that seemed to be out of control as it sped toward his fleet in an apparent suicide attack. Then as the battle continued he realized that he was losing ships at a rate that by the time the sphere was within a few thousand units he might be on the only surviving ship. His ship was strategically placed behind the back of the cone formed by all the ships in front of him.

When he gave the order for the ships to scatter and attack independently he was once again shocked as it seemed the ships randomly accelerated and crashed into another ship only to miss one and then hit another. It looked like a tournament that had been popularized were giant land moving trucks that competed to destroy each other with the winner being the vehicle that remained in operational condition.

In a few moments, his fleet was reduced to less than six ships still able to power themselves but seemed to wander through space in an uncontrolled manner.

Once again he received that hideous picture of the alien holding up an empty hand. He also received notice that he was facing execution for having performed so poorly against one small alien vessel.

He cursed on the tail of his mother and sent a picture of himself with an open claw back to the alien. He had nothing left to fight with. He got word that ground control would do the job that he had failed to do.

Tom was the one who reminded all of them of the weapon that had risen from the waters of Hurlian that he had destroyed by using the Hole cannon to put a hole through that planet. He added that he thought the weapon that had destroyed a large part of the alien fleet that they had just defeated was a similar weapon and they should get the plans for it so they could add it to the Cosmos fleet.

Elisha nodded and focused her efforts in hacking into the land based computer systems. This time she was able to insert what she referred to as a gobble routine that was not interested in what the code might be doing but simply copied it and put it into the memory cube it was associated with. She said that she would most likely get it and a ton of other information that would need to be worked on to sort out how all the alien code functioned.

18 The Jomaoko

Lydia still had the Terra at battle stations when she was informed of missiles rising from all three planets. She shook her head and ordered a systemic and continuous destruction of all the missiles that were coming out at them.

Dainoso silently observed as more than a thousand missiles rose from the three planets. He then watched as the aliens methodically eliminated them with some sort of small missile and lasers. It was clear to him that none of the missiles would reach the sphere.

Joe sent out the small fighter ships to act like tugs. There were only six alien ships that seemed to remain functional. He sent a message to the ship that had been in the rear showing a vessel retrieving the six ships. He figured the rear ship was the command ship and was rewarded by a response from that vessel.

Dainoso was surprised that he was being given the signal that he took as letting him know to rescue and survivors from his destroyed fleet. He had three rescue ships that he sent out to several of the very damaged ships. Each were soon returning with the crews of the ships that were no longer functioning. He ended up with five functional ships and his making the sixth. He had the rescued personnel distributed among the six. He had no idea how they would return to the Jomaoko until he got a message that showed small spaceships pushing each of his ships. He observed the smaller ships attach themselves to the hulls and then point each of the ships toward Jomaoko and begin what he knew would be a slow journey back to the planet.

He was surprised by both the opportunity to rescue the survivors and the fact that the aliens were taking them all back to Jomaoko. This was an act of compassion that he would not have extended if he were the conquer. It was a lesson that was humiliating but it gave him a positive impression of the weak looking aliens. He wondered what else was instore for the leadership of Jomaoko.

Joe met with the four captains and discussed how they should handle the situation.

Yara suggested that they transfer the ships back to Kelapan and turn them over to them. That would ensure they had several additional ships to protect their star system. She felt that the aliens on the planet that Elisha thought was called Jomaoko needed to be kept planet bound until sometime in the future.

Samantha suggested that several Doors get put in orbit so communication could begin and one of the older Cosmos vessels could be assigned to keep control of the planet while it could be determined if the Jomaokoans would agree to be cooperative.

Joe said that he agreed with their suggestions. He ordered the Jomaokoan ships be emptied and taken back to Kelapan. The Terra would wait in orbit until that Cosmos Ambassador got into position to control the Chieng system.

Lacey shook her head and said that she felt sorry for the ship that she loved would get such a hideous assignment.

18 The Jomaoko

Joe smiled and said that indeed it was not the top of the list of assignments but while it was on station it would hopefully not have much to do, and its personnel would be able to go on leave to many locations.

Lydia nodded and added that the Terra did not need four captains, and she was going to take the opportunity to take shore leave and was taking her Admiral with her.

19

<u>Journey to the Peak</u>

It is somewhat embarrassing, embarrassing for me, that I was one of the historians that was ignorant of his own world's history. I was proud to be a professor of history and known for my in depth knowledge of our social history. I had a published book that I proudly handed out every time I had the opportunity. Then the Admiral arrived to find a planet that had lost connection with its greatest accomplishment and me who quickly learned how superficial my knowledge was and what an ignorant individual I was. This was for me a most humbling experience.

The Admiral found Maraburo and the people on it totally ignorant about the eight planets that he had just visited and who he was organizing as part of the Intergalactic Association of Worlds. I and the people I claimed to know were totally ignorant about what the moth balled spaceship, the Kodho, had accomplished over more than nine hundred thousand years of operation. That time period numbed my soul. Nine hundred thousand years was uncomprehensible.

19 Journey to the Peak

The leaders and the people of Maraburo had forgotten that it had seeded eight planets with humans across multimillion of miles of the universe. I knew of the giant mothballed spaceship that remained in orbit around the planet, but I like everyone else had thought of it simply as relic that spoke of an opulent time when star struck individuals thought about traveling the Universe. I and my society was so self-centered that it had come to believe they were the only intelligent beings in the universe. After all the thinking was, if there were other intelligences we would surely have received a message from them after hundreds of thousands of years. Our society had for some time sent out greetings into the universe and the universe had not responded. We were sure we were a unique, rare intelligence alone in the universe and the giant relic was a display of past opulence and a time of self-grandeur.

How the Admiral reacted when he learned of the situation was very eye opening for the leadership of Maraburo and life changing for me. He engaged the leadership in casual, friendly discussion while he had his team physically visit the Kodho. They found that exterior surfaces of the ship had inches of dust and where the surface formed deeper holding areas the dust was more than six feet deep. It was not a mothballed ship it was a dead ship that for more than one hundred thousand years was in essence slowly being buried by space dust. When I think about that much dust gathering on the Kodho, I think of my ignorance being as deep.

The Maraburo leadership were in shock that the visiting sphere had humans in it and not aliens of some weird shape. They also had no idea of what the point of the visit might be. Questions like, "Were they being conquered and expected to pay some sort of ransom arose."

The Admiral made it a point to slowly educate the leaders on their history. He also had his team members on the Cosmos Terra board the Kodho. His goal was to clean and activate the ship to see if his top technical team could extract the history of the ship and by doing so the history of Maraburo.

It was then that I began my research into a man that I would find was extraordinary.

I became aware how very practical the Admiral was when I learned that unknown to anyone on Maraburo he had his eye on repurposing the Kodho as a transport ship that he would send to move the people living in fear of a dying red sun, Izuba and move the remaining people off the planet Niam to their new home in the Izulite system to the planet Nivian. I did not learn this until sometime later and then I realized the impact that the Admiral had across the nine planets of Humans and across another seven planets of intelligent non-human beings.

So, records show that the Admiral was very surprised of the memory loss of the fantastic feat of seeding eight planets around the universe over the course of almost a million years.

Yet they had kept a giant relic spaceship orbiting Maraburo that was periodically boosted back to a higher orbit because it was too big to let it fall down to the planet. He was more surprised when he and his team boarded the spaceship and were able to activate the control systems and the computers that turned out to have the history of and detailed time stamps of when each of the planets were seeded. He was especially interested in the technology that allowed the ship to structurally withstand the stresses of traveling at the speed of light. Records show that he knew intuitively that the technology of the ship that allowed for such strength was one that would make every Cosmos ship dramatically stronger than they were currently. Once again he extrapolated a new learning and enhanced the Cosmos program.

I will admit that at first I thought his actions were cavalier for taking possession of the Kodho, but my later research and my learning was that shortly after the Kodho facilitated the removal of the Nivians from their home planet to escape the red sun. He had intuitively taken the action that allowed every human on Nivia to survive. This sealed my admiration for the Admiral.

****

The ability to return to the ranch let Joe deal with his desire to move on to the visit of the last planet. The reassignment of the Cosmos Ambassador for duty at the eighth human planet, Jomaoko and then the preparation for the final journey to visit all nine planets took close to two months. Joe spent most of that time working on the ranch. It was a period that let him reflect on what he and his team had learned as they visited each of the seven other planets.

It was also a period that he kept going through a series of scenarios of what he would find when he and the team arrived at the ninth planet. A picture of a marble covered, sparkling Pyramid of Giza, the fact that his team would finally be going to the peak of the space pyramid and meet the human civilization that had the technology to seed the universe with humans played through his mind. It was hard not to be riding across the ranch and not come up with another scenario of how he would be enlightened by this final visit.

He shared this feeling with Uncle Ted and his father both of whom advised him not to expect too much and that he should not expect to find Shangri-La.

Lydia had shared many discussions with Joe about the final planet nine visit. She knew that he was expecting to learn the reason why those ancient humans had decided to seed the universe, and he was also expecting to learn about the technology that allowed them to do the seeding. Her curiosity also provided an added sense that they would learn a tremendous amount about the history of the entire human race. Joe had also talked about adding the additional fire power that they had learned about from both the eighth planet, Kelapan and the aliens on planet Jomaoko. She had made the point that the Cosmos Terra had faced them both and did not need any additional fire power and that they had become experts at Ropa-a-Dope and she was confident that the Terra and team of people that made it dance and sting were ready to face anything.

19 Journey to the Peak

The day that the Cosmos Ambassador arrived and took up an orbital position around Kelapan, Joe mentally gave a sigh of relief. He had spent the last few weeks spending time at the ranch, visiting the Cosmos facilities at Madorite and seeing how Jorge and Jerry were bringing the planet to life and discussing the technology that they had garnered from the humans on planet eight and the aliens whose death weapon was actively being reverse engineered. He felt a sense of relief to have the Ambassador take over and continue the work of establishing a working relationship with the leaders on Kelapan.

He had the Cosmos Terra return to Madorite for replenishment and preparation for what he thought of as the final journey of the Pyramid campaign. The was a journey to the source, he hoped it would fulfill at least a part of his imagined picture of a wise group of leaders and a society from which the rest of the Intergalactic human community could learn from.

The day was finally at hand for the final leg that he was thinking of as the flight up to the peak of the pyramid. He was surprised to learn from Tom and H^3 that the peak of the Pyramid of Giza was a shorter distance than the distance between that primary points at the base of the pyramid. This meant that the distance from one of the seeded planets to the peak was just slightly less than the distance between each seeded planet.

Linda smiled and said that she had consulted her numerologist that also practiced astrology and had learned that the distance to the peak divided by the distance between the eight planets predicted that the leader of the team was on the right path and that his thoughts, feelings, and instincts were aligned with the purpose of the trip to the top of the pyramid and that it marked the transition to a higher consciousness.

Yara laughed and added that if Joe believed all that she had some great property along the Amazon where he could put his hand into the clear waters and pet the fish that were smiling up at him.

Joe looked around the meeting table, shook his head and said that they were all ready to make the journey and asked Tom if he had the coordinates for the final Hole of their journey up to the top of the pyramid.

The four captains had drawn straws to see which one would take the Cosmos Terra through the Hole and Samantha had drawn the short straw.

The transition held a surprise in that all the lasers had signals flashing red, were turned, and pointing in the same direction. Samantha brought the Terra through at full battle stations ready to take hits and go into the Ropa-a-dope routine. The visual screens showed a spaceship that was at least ten times the size of any that any of them had ever seen.

Alisha was the one that let them know that the spaceship had no functioning system that she could sense.

Tom added that the ship was covered in dust and appeared to be a relic but that the planet was a very developed one that had robust activity on it.

Kashanti said that he had sent the picture of Joe with his raised hand and was waiting to see what the answer might be.

The leadership council on Maraburo had received the visual message from the what they felt was an alien craft that had mysteriously appeared a short distance from the relic Kodho spaceship. They were in disagreement in how to reply to what seemed to be an opportunistic and devious message. They decided to request the well-read professor of history, Laki Anak that had just been awarded a prize for his recent paper on how to respond if Aliens were to be contacted or were to visit Maraburo.

Laki was in the middle of writing another article on the long history of the development of the peaceful social development on Maraburo. He was in the process of digging as far back into the historical data bases that he had access to. He was aware that there were some data bases that had been archived but he didn't see a reason to try to get them unsealed. The call by the leadership council to attend the morning meeting came as a surprise. He had gone before them recently to accept an award for his paper on Aliens.

At the meeting he was shown a picture of an average looking person holding up their right empty hand. He nodded and said that was a historic sign that the person did not intend harm since his hand did not hold a weapon.

That was when the Leader sitting at the end of the table let him know that there was a spherical spaceship in orbit around Maraburo and the picture had been sent down from it.

Laki sat down and tried to recover from the shock. He had never envisioned that an Alien would look like himself. He asked why he had been called to the meeting.

The leader said that the council was asking him to be the person to decided how to deal with the aliens that looked like themselves.

Laki shook his head and replied that they should send a similar picture of the leader holding up an empty hand to let the arrivals know that there was no intention of starting a fight. Then there needed to be a way to improve communication so they could all learn how and from where the ship had originated.

Joe was relieved when he was finally shown the reply from the planet surface.

He had been looking at the ship that was floating in front of the Terra and he suddenly knew what he was going to do. He let the leadership team know that he was going to physically board the ship and see what they might find there. He named Alisha, H^3, and himself as the three lead people that would scout the ship to determine what to do next.

Lydia asked what he had in mind.

Joe smiled and said that he was going to procure another spacecraft for use in the Cosmos fleet.

19 Journey to the Peak

Joe got together with Alisha, H³ and Darian and shared what he wanted to do. He wanted Alisha to see if she could get any of the ancient control systems working if power was provided to them.. They would take over four power units to use. He asked H³ and Darian to see if they could figure out how to power up the control room. He planned to get a feel of the space and the shape the ship might be in.

It was shortly before he had scheduled the trip over to the giant ship when the reply from the planet indicating that they were also willing to be friendly was received.

He suggested that they send down a neural headset so they could establish meaningful communications. He asked that the four captains take the lead in his absence and get the communications established. He hoped that on his return he would be in the position to know how he would handle the use of the super-sized version of a lifesaving ark.

The four of them went to the spacesuit room and donned their suits. He took all of them through their safety check and then led the way to fighter craft which would serve to take them to the gigantic ship.

Alisha had been thrilled to be asked to pilot the craft. She like every crew member had qualified at flying one but she had never done so other than during that qualification processes. She really felt special to have been asked.

They began at the top of the giant craft and looked for some way that they might get on board.

Darian was the one that pointed to what seemed to be a slight depression that looked like a dimple for a super large golf ball.

When they approached H^3 put the gullwing like doors in their full vertical position and reached out and pressed on the spot. H^3 was disappointed when nothing happened.

Joe reached over and firmly tapped the spot twice. He too was disappointed by the fact that nothing happened.

Darian reached across the two of them and tapped the rhythm of shave and a haircut and laughed when a door large enough for them to go through slowly opened inward into a chamber large enough for all of them.

Alisha joked about the fact that it took three degreed Cosmos officers to open a door. She thanked them as she activated a suction anchor on the side of the ship to hold the fighter in place.

Joe stepped into the chamber and noted that it appeared to be a double entry chamber. He had all the equipment they had brought with them pulled in and when they were all in he had to physically push the outer door closed and then physically open the inner door. There was a feeling of stepping into the past as the lights on their helmets highlighted the instrumentation in that area. All four of them were pulling high energy battery packs on wheels.

Darian made the joking comment that they were only tourists arriving for their vacation and all their baggage had already passed security inspection.

19 Journey to the Peak

Once again Joe took the lead and entered a hallway that ran in the linear direction of the ship. The head lamps made it appear that the hallway in either direction ended but Joe turned to his left and walked slowly toward what he hoped would be the control room. He had no choice but to stop when the hallway ended in what appeared to be a dead end.

This time Alesha was the one that spotted a depression on the right. She tapped shave and a haircut on it, but nothing seemed to happen.

Joe realized there was no power and pushed on the area in front of him and the door pushed inward. He stepped forward and was rewarded by seeing what looked like the controls he had expected.

He turned on his more powerful one hundred thousand lumen handheld flash light and the entire room was visible.

H^3 and Darian both use their lights looking for where they thought they might find the power connection entering the room.

Darian pointed to a door that had a lightening like bolt paint in red on it. He let out a whoop when he opened it and recognized buttons that could only be breakers. He pointed to four spots on the corner of the panel.

H^3 pushed the two bottom panel buttons and Darian pushed the top two.

Together they removed the panel and put it on the floor.

H^3 commented that he did not recognize what was being used to distribute the power coming into the box but the large leads that did enter were designed to be disconnected. He proceeded to do so and added that he needed no tools to do so because the connectors had raised bumps that when press three times snapped open. Once he had them disconnected he put the leads of one of the battery packs into the clamps and snapped them closed. He counted to three and threw the switch on the battery pack. He whispered a loud, "Yes" as the lights in the control room came on.

Joe turned off his powerful flashlight and walked up to where the person guiding the craft would stand. He could see that there were windows across the front of that station. He lifted what appeared to be the top that would be found on a laptop computer and let out his breath as he was rewarded when a symbol appeared on the screen and a moment later a complete set of indicators that he was sure were giving him information about the ship lit up. All the indicators were at what he was sure indicated zero.

Alisha was down on her knees and struggling clumsily as she tried to open the console in front of her. She wanted to find a way to attach her computer and see if she could hack her way into what she was sure was a computer in the console.

Darian was randomly going around the room looking for ways to turn on the various units and other things that he had no idea what they might be. The success he had amazed all of them as the room seemed to come alive.

19 Journey to the Peak

Joe knew that they were going to be able to bring the ship to life and in short order be able to operate it. He shook his head as he thought about a technology that he was sure had operated for close to a million years and had no doubt orbited around the planet for the last hundred thousand years. This was not a gold mine it was the ultimate treasure of the human race. He absorbed the ghosts of the past million years as the realization of what they had found and what it meant overwhelmed him.

He declared their scouting trip a success and said that they should all return to the Terra.

20

More than a Gold Mine

I confess my role as the primary interface with the Admiral was a shock, and a life changing surprise. The manner of his approach was also inspirational. The first people that I and the leader of the council spoke with were the people that the Admiral utilized to introduce an unbelievable technology that immediately changed how the communications took place. It signaled to the two of us that everyone on the Admiral's team seemed to have the same status. The person calling himself Kashanti began the communication with placards and pictures, but it became clear that two headsets that appeared similar to the ones used by gamers were being sent down. He was effective in showing the headset being put on myself and on the leader of the council. The meeting ended when a messenger entered and let us know that a parachute was coming down in the commons in front of the building and had a box suspended on it.

The box when opened contained two headsets that had been shown in the pictures that were shown a few minutes before.

20 More than a Gold Mine

When I slipped my head into the helmet I was shocked hear someone welcoming me and suggested that I take a deep breath as the world of Neural communication overwhelmed me. I looked up at the screen and knew instantly that the person speaking to me was known as Captain Lacey McAdam. She raised her hand and waved as she smiled. I waved back as she pointed to each of the other Captains and introduced them. It all felt so natural to be able to understand what was being, not said, and not thought but somehow just knowing.

I looked over at the Council leader and he was shaking his head and I knew he was experiencing the same thing as I. After the four Captains introduced themselves they asked that both Director Jaktus Producy and the honorable Professor Anak give them a moment so they could have their leader, Five Star Admiral Joseph Pender Elsinger, address the Maraburo Leadership Council.

The fact that the Captains knew to whom they were speaking left both of us breathless. Director Jaktus had decided that he would sit down during the brief pause. I remained standing but had my hip on the edge of the table so that I could maintain my balance. I did not trust my body for the moment.

When the Admiral came on line, his picture and the manner of his communication was polite, smooth, and pleasing. His self-confidence, his respect for those around him, and the surge of energy that seemed to come through the neural headset seemed to pick both myself and the Director up. It was a bit like being intoxicated.

He explained that this was the ninth planet populated by humans and it was unique in that it was the planet that had seeded the other eight. He expanded his explanation to share that Maraburo was the source of all the humans that had been seeded across the universe during the past nine hundred thousand years.

I was dumb struct. Now I had to sit down too. I was a historian that for the first time was learning the actual, rich, and exceedingly long period of time that Maraburo had existed. It was then I realized that I did not deserve to be called a historian. I was a neophyte. That thought must have reached the Admiral's mind because he smiled and said that he too had trouble thinking in terms of a million years of history but he was sure that the computer data bases on the Kodho seeding ship would provide the details.

Let me say that the Admiral visually impressed the entire council. Director Jaktus later inquired if there was any organization that had such sharp and impressive looking uniforms.

Upon completing his introduction, he said good day and the Admiral took off his neural headset. The meeting was closed by Captain Lydia Tabata-Elsinger who made follow up meeting arrangements with me. It was after the call ended that I realized she was the Admiral's spouse.

I was in need of a shot of self-confidence and I wanted to personally recall all the books that I had previously proudly handed out. It was then that I started the rich and rewarding research into the Admiral's many accomplishments.

****

20 More than a Gold Mine

Joe was met by Lydia on his return from the giant derelict ship to the Terra. She let him know that they had paused the meeting with the people on planet because they wanted him to be the one that introduced the fact that the planet that she now knew was called Maraburo was the source of all the humans spread throughout the universe. She made the point that the current leadership had no memory of that accomplishment and they had no idea that the huge spaceship that orbited their planet had been the vehicle that had accomplished that feat.

Joe shook his head. He hoped that the technology that allowed that ship to traverse the distances that it had was stored on computers on board the ship and he hoped that his team would be able to find that information.

On their return, Elisha, H^3 and Darian removed their suits and went immediately to one of the conference rooms.

Once there each of them fired up their lap tops and got ready to explore the giant ships control and computer systems.

Elisha was rewarded when she was able to connect to the computer she had left on the ship. It seemed that the ship's system had interrogated her computer and approved it. She was able to locate the table of records and fields that stored the information of the technical topics and about the history of the seeding. She was not sure but she thought that perhaps even the names of the people that were seeded were in the computer records. She was rewarded with a very comprehensive table. It was large enough that she knew that a whole team could spend years digging out information.

She guided Darian to the location of how the ship that she had learned was called the Kodho was piloted. She took H^3 to the files where the specifications for the ship were stored. It quickly became clear to her that the two were figuring out how fast the ship could go.

H^3 was fascinated by the mathematical theories that he was uncovering that dealt with how to reduce the mass of the ship so as it approached the speed of light its mass would remain constant. By doing this the ancient humans had figured out how to keep the energy required at the speed of light from sky rocketing towards infinity. He wondered if he would ever be able to understand the math. He was sure that the traditional concepts that he had of front and back and that of resistance would need to be rethought if a ship the size of the Kodho was able to do so. It was just mind blowing.

Darian was interested in the type of fuel and what the constituent materials were. He was sure a ship of that size would need a tremendous amount and he was also sure it would be composed of something that they currently had no clue on how to make. As he reviewed the records, he was shocked to find out that of all things it was water!

Elisha focused her efforts in learning about the travels of the ship. She was able to determine the timing of the seeding of each planet and the time it took to seed all eight of the planets. Even at the speed of light the seeding had taken several life times of the crews that had done the seeding. It had taken the humans of that time not millions of years that she, Darian, H^3 and Joe had been thinking it had but it had taken the seeders at least a lifetime per seeding.

20 More than a Gold Mine

The seeding teams had operated the ship for more than a thousand years before putting the ship to sleep. So, the planets were seeded in roughly a one thousand year time span.

The ship had, however, been orbiting the planet for the last seven hundred thousand years. She knew that she would be working with Joe to reconcile their original belief that there was one hundred thousand years between seeding. The overall time frame was the same it was the time lines and the speed of advancement of each seeded planet that was in need of rethinking. It highlighted for her how difficult it was to get a handle on time and social change. There was no constant relationship between them that existed.

Joe entered the communication room in full dress uniform. He knew his role was to sway the leadership of the world that he had originally expected to enrich his personal understanding of the human history. Instead, he quickly realized that the seeding world had in effect suffered global dementia and forgotten their children. He knew that his team would soon have all the information that resided on the Kodho. He prepared himself as he put his cap down and slipped on the neural headset. Laki's and Jaktus's thoughts came into his mind.

He introduced himself and explained that he had grown up on the planet known as Earth. He went on to share that he and his team had been travelling the universe locating the human worlds that had been seeded by the long ago people of Maraburo. He stopped for a moment to allow Laki to share what was being said with the other members of the leadership team.

He gave a brief description of each of the eight seeded worlds. He was just about to share the timing of the seedings when Elisha interrupted him and let him know that the timing did not fit. He smiled as he processed the interruption and thanked her.

Laki was trying to maintain his composure as he took in what the Admiral was saying. He was both visually and mentally overwhelmed. He kept staring at the five stars on the shoulder patch on the Admirals uniform wondering what that meant. He must have broadcast that because Captain Tabata chuckled and replied that it meant that there was no one any higher in the command structure than the Admiral who was known as a Five Star Admiral. She went on to explain that Kpakpan was a star. Laki and Jaktus both thanked her for the explanation.

Joe then explained that he and his team had traveled from Earth the last planet to be seeded and visited each of the eight seeded planets and they now had the honor to visit the seeding planet. He then informed the leadership council that his ship the Cosmos Terra would remain in orbit for as long as it took to embrace the people on Maraburo and have them join the Intergalactic Association of Worlds where they would have the lead seat.

Laki knew that this was a surprise to all of the leadership team. He was surprised when Director Producy said that he looked forward to that honor. He asked who had invented the headset that allowed them to speak so easily.

Joe smiled and responded that it was the product of the sixth planet Keterubah. He said that it indeed had made a significant contribution. He then said that he wanted to immediately activate the Kodho and use it to save the humans on the second planet. They were in the process of moving to a new planet as their dying sun turned red and was expanding out towards it. He asked for their consent and then blanked his mind.

Laki was caught by surprise and noted that Director Producy was also caught by surprise. He decided to speak up. He shared the request with the leadership council and reminded them that the ship was a constant threat as its declining orbital height threatened the planet. He suggested that they support making the ship a part of the Admiral's Fleet of Cosmos vessels. It could in the future be a place where their young people could go to learn about the galaxy. He smiled and suggested that they name the ship the Cosmos Kodho. He was pleased to get the support of Director Producy.

Joe had allowed the discussion of the Maraburo leadership team to follow its normal routine and he was very pleased with the outcome. He informed them that the need was so pressing that though he would remain on the Cosmos Terra, he was immediately having the Cosmos Kodho moved into position to move the people of Niam with its expanding red sun moved to Nivian where they were building a new world. He made the point that the need was dire and immediate. He then suggested that they schedule daily short meetings every afternoon for the next full cycle of the travel around Kpakpan.

At the end of the meeting Joe excused himself and said that he was going to get into something more comfortable but he would like to meet with the extended team in an hour.

Lydia came on and closed the meeting with the Maraburo council and got the meeting time set.

She then called a meeting of that captains and asked for a detail up date of what they had learned. At the meeting she asked Elisha to get all the information on the Cosmos Kodho organized and put on information cubes.

Joe informed Lydia, Samantha, Yara, Lacey that they would be taking turns being Captains on the Kodho. He had been informed that the red sun had accelerated its expansion and there was a need to accelerate the removal of the people from Niam to Nivian. He then ordered all Doors that they had on board be mounted inside the Kodho and get used to make the transition even more productive by over loading the ship at Niam and then during transition at light speed continuously send people through the door until the ship was empty. He wanted to triple the current rate of people leaving the planet. He shared that he had already ordered all cosmos ships to do something similar. He shared that the human stream to Nivian was now flowing at full throttle and there was concern that it would not be fast enough.

He asked H^3, Linda and Tom to figure out what the fuel needed for the Kodho was composed of and to inform Jorge and Jerry to get it ready. He also wanted Tom to figure out how to optimize the use of the Hole cannon to optimize and increase the speed of removing people from Niam.

20 More than a Gold Mine

Tom, H^3 and Linda almost immediately figured out a way to dramatically increase the rate of removal by using the Hole cannon to fire a hole from Niam in a radial pattern that brought the Cosmos ships out a short distance from Nivian. Then the Doors placed around Nivian acted as continuous flowing conduits to move people to the surface. They commented that it would be like the Berlin airlift operation only much larger and on a global scale. They said that the Nivian planet needed to prepare the infrastructure to support the influx of the remaining millions that would arrive on a daily basis. In a month they moved more than a billion people but even then it looked like the expanding dying sun was going to roast a good portion of the people on Niam.

Every Door that existed was put into use transporting people from the surface of Niam in an attempt to save them. The concerted effort was down to the last millions of people. The use of the Kodho provided the incremental surge that was needed to save every Niamian.

The Kodho continuously left the planet packed to the hilt carrying in excess of one hundred fifty thousand on a trip and the trips continued day and night for more than six months. It moved more than thirty million people off the planet.

Lydia was loading the ship that for certain seemed to be the last flight. The red sun was pulsing and the astronomers were predicting a gigantic explosion at any moment. The people they were loading were that last remaining on the planet.

Esoteric Journey

The last shuttle load of people was landing on the Kodho and as soon as it approached Lydia had the Kodho starting to move. As the shuttle pulled in and got anchored she pushed the ship to its max. It was well beyond its maximum weight capacity and was shuttering and threatening to break up when suddenly the red star's explosion wave seemed to throw the ship forward as if it was riding the largest wave that had ever hit the North shore on Oahu. Lydia imagined looking down the wave tube and pushed the throttle well beyond maximum. She was not sure that the shuttering Kodho was going to hold together. She had every on board Door pushing people through to any Door that they could access. As the bodies left the ship, it sped up just fast enough to keep riding ahead of the wave that was trying to catch it from behind.

Lydia knew that at any moment she was going need to give the rocket engines a break. She had the Kodho going as close to the speed of light that it had ever been. It was then that she realized that the expansion of the sun had reached its maximum and she brought the ship down to ninety percent of the speed of light. During the run the ship had shed more than a million people via the Doors and the remaining people were still standing like tightly packed sardines. Every remaining human on the planet had made it on board, had held people on their shoulders when there was no room to stand.

Lydia continued the rapid movement via the Doors but she let out a breath of relief. She had tears in her eyes as she realized that she would get another chance to ride the range with Joe. She had been sure that the trip she had been experiencing was going to be her last run. She sat down and gave her second control of the ship.

Joe was still on the Cosmos Terra but had been following the flight of the Kodho. He let Yara know that he was leaving the ship and went through a Door to a Door on the Kodho. He arrival surprised everyone and as the word spread who had just arrived a hush fell and followed him to the control room. He walked in and went over to where Lydia was sitting and gave her a hug. A moment later Lacey arrived and let Lydia know she had the helm. Joe took Lydia by the hand and walked back to the Door on the way the entire Kodho reverberated with shouts of thank you. Joe told the operator the coordinates he wanted.

Lacey had taken the initiative on her own when she heard that Joe had left the Terra. She knew that it had been a moment in Joe's leadership life that had taken him to the limit as it seemed that he was about to lose Lydia.

The arrival of Joe and Lydia at the ranch was unexpected. Uncle Ted was surprised to see Lydia walk out of the Door shed followed by Joe.

Trey stood up and said that Ted should bring the bottle of Muscato to the porch.

Lydia smiled and shook her head and said that she just wanted a glass of Pelligrino with a wedge of lemon.

Joe said that he would also just have what Lydia was asking for.

Trey knew he was watching his son at a moment of high emotion. He wondered what had happened for the two of them to arrive unannounced.

The Kodho continued its flight sending people through the doors as fast as possible and by the time they began to slow to a cruising speed that would allow them to go into orbit around Nivian the ship had sent more than half of the people that had been aboard to the planet.

Lacey put the ship into orbit and turned the ship over to the support pilot.

She decided that she would visit the ranch. It had been a very emotional moment for her as well and all she could think of was to have one of Uncle Ted's steaks and one of his salty Margaritas. She knew that the planet Niam no longer existed and whatever life had been abandoned there had perished. She was aware that every species of animal had been brought out. In fact, some slithering snakes and other creatures had been around her feet as she walked to the Door to leave. She had no idea where all the people had gone or what was being done with all the creatures that had been brought out. She was also aware that a ton of materials, manufacturing equipment, and millions of pounds of food that had been abandoned as the sun expanded at an unexpected rate.

20 More than a Gold Mine

She was very aware that the four captains were all stressed out to the limit. Not long after her arrival it did not surprise her to have Yara and Samantha arrive with their mates.

She smiled when Joe repeated that the Kodho had served as more than a gold mine. She wondered what its fate was destined to be.

21

<u>Completion and Next Steps</u>

The closing of the Admiral's journey to my planet was not the highlight I expected it would have been because of what followed when the Kodho was absorbed into the Admiral's fleet. I followed the use of the Kodho with a tremendous sense of pride after all I had grown up looking up at what was to all Maraburoans a light in the night sky as large as a white melon held in one's hand. When at the last moments it saved close to half a million people from an exploding star and was itself on the verge of being destroyed by it, I was at the edge of my seat as it fought to stay ahead of the star's forceful wave of energy that seemed to be trying to swallow the ship. When the Kodho finally broke free I had tears in my eyes as I thought about the team that the Admiral had around him. I personally wished I could have been part of that team.

I have instead become an influencer that has detailed all of the Admiral's journeys. I continue to follow him wherever he journeys and this means that I am now constantly traveling Door to Door like the proverbial shoe salesman on Earth.

21 Completion and Next Steps

I have personally traveled to every Door that orbits the eight seed planets and I have started my second cycle as the Doors on the planet themselves are opened for travelers. My goal is to visit all eight planets and document the histories that each holds. It is a historian's dream come true and it is a bigger quest then I will ever be able to finish during my life time. However, I will leave historical journal after historical journal not only about the things I see and learn but about what the Admiral and his team continues to do.

It was of interest to me when I learned that the Admiral had put the Kodho to use as a transport of material from the planets located in the Izulite system to accelerate the transformation of the Nivian planet. I found it fitting that it continued to be of use even as a lowly freighter. After all that was a much better fate then orbiting a planet of people ignorant of its greatest achievement. The history that it had preserved allowed me to clearly document the greatness to which Maraburo had risen at one time. It helped me to set a new goal of leading the people that it had sent out to establish new worlds to know and understand the rich history that had been made. I was honored to be selected to be a member of the Intergalactic Association of Worlds which provides me the means to fulfill that goal.

That position has allowed me to continue to follow the journeys that the Admiral continues to go on. I has also allowed me to expand my horizon as that organization enrolls the beings that we called aliens but other than body shape differences most often have similar social desires as humans.

Esoteric Journey

My life has achieved heights that I, in the past, would never have dreamt possible and I clearly attribute those heights to the Admiral.

****

The veranda on the ranch was a buzz with Joe's team celebrating having been able to save the people of Niam and of getting them all to Nivian. They all agreed that the final surge by every Cosmos vessel including the hastily commissioned Kodho to get the people off Niam was the greatest achievement of their years long journeys across the universe as they visited the human populated planets.

Lacey made a toast to Lydia and the final flight that was almost swallowed by a red exploding star that seemed determined to eat it. The veranda reverberated to the repeated Voya, Voya, Voya that surely must have frightened the horses and the cattle that were around the ranch.

Lydia could not help but break down into tears. She lifted her glass of wine and said that her first love was Joe, her second was the Voyager, her first command, and now she was admitting that the gigantic ship the Kodho had forever earned a place in her heart. She had never pushed a ship beyond its limits like she had just pushed it. She said that she could still feel it shuddering as she pushed it beyond its design limits in an attempt to be able to hold her first love once again in her arms. She dried her tears and said that she had never cursed so much as when she was damming the red dying star for threatening to keep her from Joe's arms. She finished her wine and said that she needed to take a walk and left the veranda.

Joe followed and those on the porch watched as the two were silhouetted by the moon as the embraced and kissed.

233

Uncle Ted stood and asked who else needed another and the discussion turned back to the last surge to get people off the planet.

Tom made the point that he had never expected the Door units to process so many people so fast. He added that several of the Door units had experienced overloads and that had created hiccups in the transport process but overall, a record in the speed of transports had been set. He shared the fact that the more than fifty units that had been on Niam had met their fate with the rest of the planet. The cameras on those units had recorded the approaching blinding light of the sun and were sure to provide information that would help scientists learn more about the power and the speed of the final death of a star.

Elisha felt a surge of adoration for the people on the veranda. She had grown up in a poor household to caring parents that had struggled to make ends meet. Her mother had encourage her to go for the gold and pushed her academically. Her father had pushed her to be herself, not be pushed around and supported her in all her team sports. She had from the start liked to use her knack in the use of computers to see if she could hack into the programs that she had access to. She got a degree in computer science with a focus on programming. She learned to be an invisible hacker meaning that she practiced hacking in such a way that the hacked program did not realize it had been hacked.

She might someday let Lydia know that she had been with her on that electrifying escape from the dying star. She had removed the override the limits of the power control system. She had monitored the warning signals and had overridden the engine shutdown commands. The reason that the entire structure of the Kodho went into vibration was that it was more than fifty percent beyond all of its design parameters. The engines were on the verge of exploding but she had overridden the cut off commands. Lydia and the people on the Kodho all had traveled faster than the speed of light and in doing so had out run the dying sun!

She took a long sip of her drink as she thought about what she had done she also knew that she wanted to dig into every aspect of what made up the Kodho. She knew that there was more to the engineering of that vessel than had so far been learned. She was going to continue digging but for now she was happy having been included in the gathering on the ranch. She knew that the invitation from Joe meant she was now part of his team.

Joe indeed knew that Elisha had been involved in Lydia's escape from the voracious exploding star. He had observed Elisha frantically typing away on her computer, shaking her head, taking in and holding her breath, then letting out low moans and again typing furiously. This was at the same time that he was observing Lydia at the controls of the ship doing almost the same thing. He wondered which of the two were actually controlling the ship. He concluded by their synchronized physical displays that they were both doing so.

He would eventually learn what Elisha had been doing but he knew that she would have been manipulating the control systems of the ship. He now had his eye on Elisha to be a key player in his future journeys.

Darian had his hand on Samantha's as he sipped on some of the apple cider that he had made. He knew that Samantha identified with what Lydia had just experienced. All four of the Captains had taken turns at the helm of the Kodho in the valiant effort to save the people on Niam. It had been six months of frantic effort to extract as many people as possible. The Kodho was over capacity on every trip away from the planet. The four captains rotated on a weekly basis and each time Samatha was exhausted from the stress she faced in moving at a breakneck speed. He had listened to her describe the red bubble which the star had turned into visually moving toward the planet.

He knew from personal observations on the telescopes on the Cosmos Terra that from a distance that the death of Izuba looked more like a four spiked three dimensional red rectangle that had a very bright center and was not a bubble. He had observed the glowing red expanding gas and dust as it surged towards Niam and the rapid formation of the dense white dwarf even as Samantha, Lydia, Yara and Lacey raced to extract all the people. He had personally suffered repeated emotional attacks that affected him more than the day he had been diagnosed with terminal cancer. He was drinking the apple cyder that he had made following Samantha's mix of apples because it was the one drink that focused his mind on how much he loved her.

Yara had previously survived the total destruction of the Odessey. She knew that she was sitting on the veranda of the home that Joe had grown up in because of his consistent demand that the ship that she commanded pass maneuvering tests that stretched all personnel to the limit. She had become an ardent believer in his intuitive ability to foresee what the team needed next. She had been surprised by his rapid assimilation of the Kodho and its use to extract the people from Niam. Each turn she took at the helm of the ship became more stressful as she visually saw the approaching red front from the dying star. Each captain took the helm for a one week period. Her turn had been the week before Lydia's and she had experienced the anxiety of the people that were last to be leaving. She had also experienced the personal stress as it seemed that she was literally flying into the star itself. It was hard for her to comprehend how Lydia had been able to take on more than double the number of people on that last run and then still be able to stay ahead of the gas bubble that reached the planet even as the ship struggled to escaped the grasp of the hot gases. She understood Lydia's comments and personally felt the emotion that she had expressed.

Joe had asked her to the ranch. Jackie knew that he was concerned about the stress he had put his four captains through during the last six months. She was observing first hand as that stress manifested itself in the discussion on the veranda. She had previous sessions with everyone but Lacey. She knew that Samantha, Yara and Lydia had the partner's that provided the support that would help them recover from the stress that they had just endured.

21 Completion and Next Steps

She planned to spend most of her time with Lacey, who she sensed had been stressed but who was a person who had years of dealing with top level stress. After all, one does serve two terms as President, then step into the role of Intergalactic Ambassador and finally settle into becoming a Cosmos spaceship captain and not be ablet to deal with stress. It was also clear to her that Lacey, though stressed by recent events was leading the recovery effort by turning it into a group discussion.

Jackie knew that the person that was the hardest to diagnose was Joe. She had first tried to diagnose him when he had volunteered to be one of the first three humans to transit through the Door. Lydia was the first and was totally cured of her cancer. Darian was second and Joe was third. Darian was an easy diagnosis who until he met Samantha was on the way to becoming a womanizer.

Joe was as stoic as she had later learned his father was. It was very hard to know what he was thinking or if he was under stress. She knew that Joe had most likely suffered the most stress by the situation he had put Lydia in. She had never met two people that were truly halves of a greater whole until she understood how the two functioned to strengthen each other. As she watched them holding hands, walking in the moon light across the yard she knew that they would heal each other.

Joe knew that Lydia's escape from a dying red sun was why he was still functioning. He held her hand and thought back from the first day he had arrived at Lakland as part of the Door experiment and the night before she was the first to go through the Door and he sat watching her lay on the couch asleep. He knew then that he was looking at his other half and he knew that had she not escaped the dying star, he would at the moment be following her to wherever one goes after death. He could not envision a life without her.

Tom and Linda had saved both of them by inventing the Door and he would support them for as long as they lived. He was sure that Elisha had enabled the Kodho to perform beyond anything it had been designed to do and that she had saved Lydia. He would make sure that he would support her for as long as she lived.

He also knew that the harmony that his team enjoyed was because they listened to each other and seemed to weave each other's ideas into a social fabric that rang of positive energy. As he looked up at the full silvery moon he thanked his mother for looking out for he and the people he thought of as his family.

The End

21 Completion and Next Steps

About the Author

Ronald E. Mueller
remwriter95@gmail.com

Ron grew up in what is now Flint River State Park in Southeast Iowa. The 170-year-old house Ron lived in is built into a hillside. It faces a 125-foot-high cliff towering over the little Flint River. The house and the land talked to him about; the passing of time, the struggle to conquer the land, the struggles people faced and the wonder of nature.

He climbed the cliffs, crawled into the caves, dove from the swimming rock, collected clams from the bottom of the pond, gigged and skinned frogs for their legs. He trapped muskrats for fur, hunted raccoon in the dead of night, and with only a stick hunted rabbits in the dead of winter.

His young life was outdoors, and nature tested him.

He walked to a one room stone schoolhouse uphill both ways. A stern but warm-hearted teacher, Mrs. Henry was instrumental in shaping his character as she shepherded him from the fourth to the eighth grade. A Montessori before its time. It was a wonderful way to grow up.

His experiences inter-twined with snippets of fantasy lend themselves to the adventures he leads the reader through.

Characters in the Story

Characters in the Story

Published by: Around the World Publishing LLC.

QR Links to
ATWP.US web site

243